The Other Kind : The Rise
(Extended 2nd Version)

ISBN-13: 978-93-343-9834-2

The Other Kind
Part 1: The Rise

By

Yusuf Bhatti

2025

Contents

Introduction

In a world where humanity believes itself the pinnacle of evolution, a hidden lineage thrives in the shadows—*the other kind.* For centuries, these genetically superior beings have manipulated history, cloaked in myth as jinn, witches, or angels. Governed by the Sisters' Council, a matriarchal regime born from the ashes of a catastrophic war between two ancient kings, they enforce a brutal code: *no man of their kind shall wield power again.*

But in 1996, a boy named Arham is born in Mumbai. Unaware of his heritage, he grows into a man whose superhuman strength and unyielding resilience mark him as a threat to the Sisters' centuries-old order. Hunted, tested, and thrust into a labyrinth of betrayal, Arham becomes the catalyst for a revolution that could shatter the Council's iron grip—or plunge the world into chaos.

This is a tale of immortality and rebellion, where love clashes with tyranny, and the sins of the past ignite the fires of war. Welcome to a hidden world where the line between human and superhuman is blurred, and survival demands a price darker than death.

---

* * *

Chapter 1: Bloodlines & Betrayal

For eternity, mankind has been regarded as the most evolved being in the universe—unchallenged and undisputed. Yet, in the shadows of our planet, another kind has lived for centuries. This kind evolved from humans, possessing superior genes. With access to modern technology, they have widened the gap between themselves and mankind. When humans occasionally crossed paths with them, they called them jinn, witches, magicians or even angels. They are conspicuous yet blend seamlessly into society as successful humans.

Four centuries ago, the world was ruled by men of this other kind—two kings of immense power, one controlling the east and the other the west. Their greed for dominance led to a catastrophic war. In the year 1724, the kings turned on each other, their battles decimating entire cities and leaving their people in ruins. By the time the dust settled, the kings were dead, and only the two queens remained. The kings' war had forced every person to fight, leading to a drastic decline in their population—from thousands to mere hundreds.

The queens, horrified by the destruction wrought by their husbands, vowed never to let such power fall into the hands of men again. They formed the Sisters Council, a secretive alliance dedicated to ensuring that men of their kind would never rise to power. The queens killed all remaining warrior men, and those who weren't killed were young boys who were enslaved. For these boys, their only purpose was to propagate the lineage of "the other kind" through human women, as the women of their kind could not bear children. The two queens, along with four of their most fearsome female warriors, established the Sisters Code and divided six territories among themselves to rule. The queen of the east chose to rule what is now the Europe, while the queen of the west chose to rule Americas. The remaining four warriors selected their native regions: the Indian subcontinent, Russia, the Middle east, and Africa. The most important rule of the Sisters Code was that no sister would encroach upon or conquer the territory of another.

Over time, the queens discovered the secret of blood transfusion, allowing them to extend their lives indefinitely. Leena, from the Indian subcontinent, was the youngest and most ambitious of the warriors. She was the first to master the technique, and the others soon followed. However, the Queen of the Americas—now an old, withered woman—learned too late. By the time she began her transfusions, her body had already aged beyond repair. Yet, she clung to life, her hatred for men of their kind burning brighter than ever.

Today, this tale is documented for one purpose: the other kind have been purged by someone unknown—a newborn from the other kind, yet different in so many ways.

Born in a suburb of Mumbai in 1996 to a family whose father ran a small but busy restaurant, Arham was an average student but excelled in sports. A shy and introverted boy, he had been expelled from multiple schools for fighting and injuring other kids. A skinny child who attracted bullies with his seemingly frail body and soft voice, Arham would respond with strength that could only be described as superhuman for his age. Each time he was bullied, he fought back, beating his tormentors black and blue, only to cry later in shock at the damage he had unintentionally caused. The guilt would linger as his parents struggled to find him a new school, and he had to start over, making new friends.

Arham knew he was different. Other kids were always amused by how he didn't seem to feel pain, and his retaliatory strikes were far more damaging than those of physically larger children. As he grew into his mid-teens, he learned to pull his punches and avoid causing harm, hoping to spare himself and his parents' further trouble. Yet, as the perpetual new kid, he often found himself in situations where he couldn't hold back, sometimes unleashing his anger in terrifying outbursts.

After finishing school at 18, his parents, desperate to curb his fighting, decided against college and enrolled him in a boxing gym instead. There, Arham began to experience the best days of his life. By then, he had mastered the art of pretending to feel pain, though his tolerance was extraordinarily high. He pulled his punches during training to avoid drawing attention to his inhuman strength. During sparring sessions, his coaches were impressed by his dedication and the power of his strikes, quickly advancing him to weekly beginner fights. Week after week, Arham defeated his opponents with ease, barely breaking a sweat.

After two years, he was scheduled for his first real fight without protective gear. Arham agreed without hesitation. He knocked out his opponent within seconds, landing a hard right punch to the head. The head coach, astonished, immediately pitted him against a more experienced fighter. Realizing he had been too eager in his first fight; Arham took his time in the second. He absorbed a few hits, threw fewer punches, and in the second round, grew frustrated and went for the knockout. A right uppercut broke his opponent's defence, followed by a left punch straight to the face, leaving the opponent flat on the ground.

The coaches erupted in joy, hailing him as a wonder boy who could knock out opponents with both hands. Arham smiled, pretending to be surprised, though deep down, he knew he was a freak of nature. News of the wonder kid spread through fighting clubs across the city. Defeating opponents who were physically bigger and more experienced became routine for him. Slowly but surely, he began earning modest sums from fight nights.

One day, he caught the attention of Lin, a former Muay Thai professional from Thailand. Lin offered to train Arham in Muay Thai at his dojo in Thailand, where he could learn a new fighting style and earn a steady income. Arham accepted immediately, securing his parents' permission to travel.

***

Chapter 2: Knives Don't lie

Lin lived on Fight Street in Bangkok, where he owned his own gym. Many foreigners came to learn Muay Thai and often stayed for long periods. Within a year, Arham had become a seasoned fighter with strong fundamentals in Muay Thai. By now, he was participating in fights with local professionals and had mastered the art of acting hurt and weak enough to fool everyone. Slowly, he gained popularity and was nicknamed "Punching Bag" because he would take countless hits to his body due to his inexperienced defense, yet he never got knocked out. He ended fights at his own whim and will.

Arham was content with his lifestyle and success. One night, under a full moon, he sat alone on a deserted beach around midnight, contemplating the life choices he had made. He wondered where he would be if Mr. Lin hadn't brought him to Thailand. Suddenly, on the empty beach, he heard footsteps behind him. Three men armed with knives approached—thieves demanding money and his phone.

Arham smiled at them and replied gently, "Sorry, guys, I can't help you. I'm in a happy mood right now and not in the mood to get mugged."

The thieves laughed at his response, and one of them lunged at him, stabbing toward his chest. To their shock, the tip of the knife bent upon impact. Arham laughed amusingly, as if he had been tickled. The thieves stood frozen, baffled by what had just happened. They stared at the bent knife, trying to make sense of it, while Arham glanced at his shirt, noticing the hole the knife had made.

Arham stopped laughing, his expression turning serious. "This wasn't supposed to happen," he said grimly. "Now you've witnessed something no one else has. I'll have to make sure you forget."

Before the thieves could react, Arham knocked all three to the ground with a few swift punches. He dragged them to the sea and nearly drowned them, holding two by the backs of their necks and stepping on the third in the shallow water. He continued until they were exhausted, then left them on the beach with a warning: "Never mention what happened today, or I'll find you and show no mercy."

By the age of 28, Arham was earning a steady income from fighting at local clubs and had become a permanent resident of Thailand. Still undefeated, he was a crowd favorite. By now, he had grown close to Fa Ying, a female fighter and the daughter of his mentor, Lin. Fa Ying had been training at the gym since childhood.

Arham's life revolved around the gym, where he learned from Lin, who had become a father figure to him, and spent time with Fa Ying and his gym friends at beaches and malls. Wanting to earn more so he could buy a house and move out of his small apartment near the gym, Arham decided to compete in professional fights at larger venues against the best fighters from around the world.

He was already a popular name in the local gym and club circuit, and crowds flocked to watch him fight. His matches were always a spectacle, with Arham often staging dramatic comebacks. Yet, poor Arham was naïve. His growing fame attracted attention from some who would change his life forever.

They were “the other kind”—the kind who were somewhat like him, yet different.

***

Chapter 3: The Last Act

One day, while making his way to the ring for one of the top-ranked fights of his career, Arham felt a strange energy in the hall. As he entered the ring and his name was announced, he scanned the crowd of hundreds. His eyes landed on six women, all of different ethnicities, dressed in well-tailored jackets and coats that contrasted sharply with the casual attire of the cheering crowd. Unlike the others, who were screaming at the top of their lungs, these women stared at him with expressionless faces.

Arham, ever the showman, flexed his biceps and raised his arms aggressively to pump up the crowd, all while glancing back at the women, hoping to elicit a reaction. Instead, they looked away, avoiding eye contact with him and communicating subtly with each other through body language.

The fight followed the usual script Arham had perfected over the years. To him, taking hits felt like receiving a massage. His strong bones and thick skin rendered his opponent's efforts useless. After a few rounds, when the crowd began to lose hope for him, Arham steadily turned the match around and finished with a knockout—still without using his full strength.

After the fight, the six women left immediately. Arham was astonished by their abrupt departure and asked Lin if he knew who they were. Lin brushed it off, suggesting they might have bet on Arham to lose and were disappointed by the result.

Outside the arena, the women gathered in the parking lot, standing in silence until one of them, an Indian woman, spoke up. "I believe he is one of us, and we need to act immediately," she said.

Another woman argued, "The fight looked normal. It might just be luck that he turned it around."

The Indian woman countered, "I've asked around. No one has ever seen him bleed. Yes, most of his fights are long, but he's never lost a match and always wins by knockout. He's risen through the ranks like no one else."

The others quickly agreed, deciding not to take any chances. If Arham turned out to be one of the other kind, they would be held accountable for failing to act.

That night, as Arham left the gym late, he was stopped by a police officer who asked for his identification. After showing his ID, he was told to come to the police station for interrogation, as he matched the description of a suspect in a crime. Arham refused, saying he was tired after a long day and would come the next morning. To his surprise, the officer agreed.

Arham walked toward his apartment, but as he reached his door, he realized the police officer had followed him. Suddenly, a van pulled up, and several men shot Arham multiple times with a gun while one of them recorded the incident with an old camcorder. They fled immediately, leaving Arham lying on the ground.

Despite the impact of the bullets, Arham felt no pain and didn't bleed, except for a few minor marks left by the bullets. He looked around and noticed the police officer was nowhere to be found.

Fa Ying, who had been in the lobby of Arham's apartment building, witnessed the shootout through the glass door. She ran to Arham, shocked to find no blood on him. Arham quickly made an excuse, saying it was a silly prank with fake guns.

As he sat up, Arham realized someone was aware of his superhuman abilities and had tested him by recording the incident. He had no enemies, so this was clearly a calculated move. Hearing ambulance sirens in the distance, Arham rushed to his apartment, applied red paint to his chest to mimic blood, and waited, hoping to lure out whoever was behind this.

Three paramedics arrived and, without being directed, went straight to Arham's apartment. They placed him on a stretcher but didn't administer any medicine or IV. They simply told him to lie still until they reached the hospital.

The ambulance took Arham to an isolated area with nothing but a makeshift single-room structure. Inside, Arham noticed surveillance cameras. The paramedics left him on the bed, saying a doctor would arrive shortly.

A few moments later, Arham heard a clicking sound under the bed. He lifted the sheet and found an explosive device. He bolted out of the room just as the explosion went off, flinging him a few meters away. His clothes were burnt, and his skin was blackened and sore.

As he struggled to stand, he heard tires screeching and saw the paramedics speeding away in the ambulance. Suddenly, a light approached from the distance—it was Fa Ying on her scooter. She had followed the ambulance but was left behind. The explosion had drawn her to the scene.

Together, they left the area and returned home.

---

* * *

Chapter 4: Hunting My Killers

The next day, Arham began searching for the police officer who had stopped him the night before. He visited every police station in the area over the next two weeks but found no trace of the man. It became clear that the officer was not real cop. Desperate for answers, Arham enlisted the help of a hacker friend to track the license plates of the shooters' van and the ambulance. However, all the plates turned out to be unregistered or fake.

Realizing the only way to find his attackers was to lure them out, Arham advertised his next fight in the local newspaper, challenging the reigning champion. The plan worked. That same night, the fake cop, the paramedics, and the shooters were waiting for him outside his apartment building.

They confronted him, their confusion evident. "We shot you, and you were bleeding. Your clothes were drenched in blood. We saw you burn in the explosion. How are you alive?" one of them demanded.

Arham smiled calmly. "I'll explain everything. Let's sit somewhere, have a drink, and talk."

They laughed but agreed, gesturing for him to get into their van. They drove to a Vietnamese restaurant in Chinatown, entering through a separate back entrance into a private room adorned with gang signs. Arham realized he was dealing with members of a Vietnamese gang.

They seated him and handed him a glass of water. One of the gang members sneered, "Okay, here's your drink. Now, tell us how you're alive and in perfect condition."

Arham leaned back in his chair, relaxed. "That's the wrong question, my friend. Let me ask the right one: Who hired you to kill me? And remember, your answer will decide whether you live or not."

The gang members exchanged glances, then arrogantly replied, "We're Vietnamese gang members. We do what our boss tells us to do."

Arham nodded. "Where can I find your boss?"

"In Capital Bangkok Prison," one of them said mockingly. "What are you going to do now? Commit a crime, get yourself arrested, and take revenge?"

Arham smiled. "Oh yeah, I'm going to commit a crime now—and you're all going to be the victims."

The gang members were taken aback. They had already been curious about how Arham had survived, but his confidence now made them rethink their approach. One of them finally spoke up. "We brought you here to kill you, but since you have a death wish to go to prison where our boss is held, we'll take you there ourselves. You'll enter as a prisoner at our command, and leaving won't be an option."

Arham agreed without hesitation.

---

* * *

Chapter 5: Prison Break

Upon reaching the police station, the gang members instructed Arham to confess to an unresolved murder. Arham complied, and after admitting to the crime, he was taken into custody and spent the night in jail. The next morning, he was transferred to Capital Prison in Bangkok.

Arham was led through a tunnel to an underground basement within the prison. At the end of the tunnel was a cell with steel bars instead of walls, allowing him to see into a larger holding area on the other side. The prisoners were kept in a large room, separated from him by a steel gate guarded by prison officers. Arham was asked to pass through a scanning machine to ensure he carried no weapons. He was then handed a prisoner's uniform to change into.

As Arham removed his shirt, he noticed all the prisoners staring at him, waiting on the other side of the gate. An old man stepped forward and said, "So, you're the fool who willingly admitted to murder just to see me. I must be special."

Arham realized this was the boss of the Vietnamese gang. He replied, "I'm no enemy of yours. I just want to know why you wanted me dead. I don't even know you."

The boss smirked. "I've been promised freedom from this prison if I kill you."

Arham narrowed his eyes. "By whom? Who's offering you freedom?"

The boss shrugged. "That's not your concern. Once you step through this gate, you'll face a painful death. These prisoners work for me, and they're willing to kill or die if necessary."

Arham closed his eyes, looked down, and said calmly, "Your gang outside made a wise decision by not fighting me and bringing me here. I'll give you one last chance to save yourself. Tell me who hired you, or this prison will be flooded with blood today."

The boss laughed arrogantly. "Then open the floodgates. I'll wait."

The prisoners behind him began chanting, "Flood blood! Flood blood!" trying to taunt Arham. Even the guards joined in, mocking him. Arham glanced at the guard beside him, who was still holding his uniform and taunting him. In one swift motion, Arham shoved the guard into the steel wall, knocking him unconscious. He then charged at the two guards by the gate, slamming them into the bars with such force that they too fell unconscious.

The prisoners fell silent, their taunts replaced by fear. The boss, now visibly nervous, retreated behind the group and shouted, "One million Thai baht to whoever kills him!"

Arham pressed the button to open the gate and stepped into the larger compound. Unbeknownst to the prison staff, the security cameras in the control room were looping footage of Arham talking to the boss. Before entering the prison, Arham had ensured his hacker friend manipulated the security feed.

Arham sprinted toward the group of prisoners and pushed the first one with full force. The man flew through the air, crashing into four others behind him. The first prisoner was barely breathing, and the others were too terrified to attack.

Seeing this, the boss yelled, "Five million baht and freedom from prison for life to whoever kills him!"

The prisoners rushed at Arham, but he was unstoppable. He punched, kicked, and elbowed his way through, killing several instantly. Realizing he didn't want to kill them all, he changed tactics, picking up prisoners and hurling them into the crowd. Despite their numbers, they couldn't overpower him.

Suddenly, the prisoners stopped attacking. Arham turned to see around 50 prison guards in riot gear, armed with shields and metal rods, entering the compound. They positioned themselves between Arham and the mob boss.

Arham realized the surveillance room hack had been discovered. Knowing he had to act fast before his actions were recorded, he leaped over the guards, landing behind them. He began throwing and slamming them into each other and the walls, incapacitating all of them within minutes.

The boss, now panicked, stood up and revealed, "The morning before you were attacked, two women of Indian origin visited me. They placed a bounty of ten million baht on your head."

Arham had suspected the women were behind this, and now he had confirmation. He grabbed a riot shield and forced his way to the surveillance room. Upon arriving, he searched for footage of the women's visit but found it missing. Enraged, he destroyed the room by setting it on fire and fought his way out of the prison, overpowering anyone who stood in his path.

As he emerged from the prison, a car pulled up in front of him. The back door opened, revealing a well-dressed man in a white suit. "Hello, brother Arham," the man said. "Get in, and I'll take you to the people who want you dead."

Arham frowned. "Who are you, and how do you know my name?"

The man replied, "Leave any electronics you're carrying on the ground and get in the car. All your questions will be answered."

---

* * *

Chapter 6: Queen's Bargain

Upon entering the car, Arham asked again, "Who are you?"

The man replied, "You can call me Hamid. I'm here on behalf of my queen. I've been ordered to take you to her. For the safety of both myself and my queen, I cannot reveal any more names or information about where we're going." Hamid's accent and demeanour suggested he was from the Middle East.

They travelled for an entire day, eventually reaching an abandoned airstrip in the middle of nowhere. There, they boarded a small private jet and flew through the night, landing on another airstrip in the middle of a desert. The buildings were camouflaged, with no markings or flags, giving the appearance of a secret military base. From there, Arham was driven to a remote beach mansion.

Hamid instructed Arham to rest, assuring him that the queen would visit him personally soon. In the mansion, Arham was assigned a butler who would provide him with food and anything else he required. Hamid explained that the staff members were stationed at the back of the mansion and that Arham was to stay in the front section, avoiding contact with anyone except the butler. "The fewer people who know of your presence here, the better," Hamid said. He also warned Arham not to venture outside or onto the shore for safety reasons. Arham agreed.

The next morning, Hamid returned to inform Arham that the queen had arrived and would see him now. He escorted Arham to a small room in the mansion where the queen sat alone. She was an elderly Middle Eastern woman with white hair, seated in a chair by the corner of the room, gazing at the ocean through a glass façade. Hamid gestured for Arham to sit in the chair beside her and then left the room.

The queen turned to Arham and asked, "Would you like some tea or coffee?"

Arham replied politely, "No, thank you. I've been well taken care of since I arrived."

The queen nodded and began, "My son, I am the queen of my country, yet no one knows of my existence except a few. I've lived a quiet life and never thought I would meet a man of our kind. We are unique, my son. We are 'the other kind'—human, yet so much more. Our kind is gifted with strength beyond that of any living being. I know you have many questions, and I am here to answer each one."

Arham quickly asked, "How many of us exist? And who is trying to kill me?"

The queen replied, "I don't know the exact number, but we are very few—perhaps no more than a few hundred. The one trying to kill you is also a queen, like me. She goes by the name Leena. She commands a small army of women of our kind, whom she calls her daughters. They refer to her as 'Mother.' Leena is a dangerous and evil woman. Her daughters work as secret agents, infiltrating the governments of most first-world countries and manipulating them for monetary gain. She also controls many advanced technology and surveillance firms. They must have discovered you through one of your fights and realized you are one of us. They see all men of our kind as threats to their supremacy and will not let you live. They underestimated you by hiring humans to kill you, but now that you've survived, her daughters will hunt you down themselves. The only way to survive is to strike first—cut off the head of the snake. Kill Leena. But be cautious; she is incredibly powerful. The only way to kill her is through a sneak attack—cut off her head and remove her heart. I will guide you to her, but you must do the killing."

Arham shook his head. "You're mistaken. I may be a fighter, but I'm not a killer. Take me to her, and I'll convince her that I mean no harm."

The queen fell silent for a moment, the room filled with tension. After a while, she said, "Women of our kind lack reproductive organs, so we cannot give birth. Only a man of our kind and a human woman can produce offspring of our lineage. Leena's daughters were either taken from their families or born through a breeding program. She keeps a few men as prisoners, using them to propagate more of our kind. Leena is over 400 years old and has been using her daughters as blood banks and organ donors to maintain her immortality. I'm not sure if her daughters are aware of this evil, but even if they are, they are too weak to rebel against her. You, however, are strong and a trained fighter. She won't risk imprisoning you—she'll try to kill you. But you must strike first and end her. Most men of our kind are imprisoned or killed young to prevent them from becoming threats to her."

Arham was stunned. "So, you want me to sneak up and kill a 400-year-old blood-stealing mother who has an army of our kind protecting her? This is insane. I didn't come here to hurt an old woman, let alone kill one. I need time to process all of this."

The queen called for Hamid, who brought a sword and handed it to Arham. The queen explained, "This weapon can pierce the skin of our kind. It's made from the strongest material—unbreakable and unbendable."

Arham replied confidently, "You can keep it. I only trust my guns, and they're attached to my body—my left hand and my right hand."

The queen smiled. "As you wish, my son."

Hamid added, "Leena can't be tracked or traced. We don't know where she lives or what she or her daughters look like. We only know the location of her investment company's office in Málaga, Spain. You'll need to infiltrate it to retrieve information about her or her daughters' whereabouts. Even if we capture one of her daughters, we can use her to track Leena. I'll take you to Spain whenever you're ready. I'll keep the sword with me in case you need it. But remember, if you're captured, you must never mention us, or she'll wipe out our entire lineage."

Arham smirked sarcastically. "Thanks for letting me know no one has my back."

***

Chapter 7: Daggers in Daylight

A few days later, Arham was informed that the plan was ready. He was driven back to the airfield and flown to Spain with Hamid. Arham remained confident that matters wouldn't escalate further and that he could eventually negotiate peace with the mother.

Hamid briefed Arham on the plan: An investor from a foreign country was visiting the office for the first time, and Arham would replace a local consultant in the investor's entourage. Once inside the building, Arham was to discreetly separate from the group and search for the daughters. "We don't know their identities," Hamid explained, "but you're the only one who's seen them ringside. If you find one, send us a text with her exact floor and room number, then leave immediately. My team will track her until she meets the mother. When that happens, you'll do what's necessary."

Arham asked, "What if she sees and recognizes me?"

Hamid joked, "Use your weapons—whatever they are—and leave the building immediately. Meet us at the rendezvous point, and make sure you're not followed. Remember, if you're caught, you've never met me or the queen. And by the way, Hamid isn't my real name."

The next day, the meeting was scheduled. Arham joined the investor's entourage and entered the building. They were guided to a conference room, and while waiting, Arham excused himself and stepped out. As he opened the door, he saw the Indian woman from the ringside walking toward him with a group of people. Panicking, he returned to his seat, hoping she hadn't noticed him.

She entered the room with her team and began introducing herself, greeting each person. When she reached Arham, she paused momentarily, clearly surprised to see him. The meeting started at 12:30 PM and lasted until 1:00 PM. Throughout, the woman kept glaring at Arham with visible rage. Arham sat quietly, unsure whether to leave or stay.

When the meeting ended, everyone stood up and exchanged farewells. As Arham was about to leave, the woman approached him and said, "Hello, sir. I have some queries. Can you wait for a moment to discuss them?"

Arham agreed and sat back down. Once everyone had left, the woman made a call and instructed the staff to take the rest of the day off. Arham, watching through the glass as the employees left, realized he should have left when he had the chance.

The woman sat quietly, texting on her phone. Arham finally asked, "So, madam, what's the query you wanted to discuss?"

She snapped, "Shut up."

Arham stood to leave, but she said, "Where do you think you're going? Look around—I've cleared the floor. Look outside—I've vacated the entire premise. Sit down. I have a surprise for you."

Arham replied sarcastically, "It's not my birthday, and I don't like surprises."

She smirked. "Oh, no, no. You misunderstood. We're celebrating your death day, not your birthday."

Arham asked, "How long do I have to wait for this delusional surprise?"

She checked her phone and said, "Just five more minutes, love. Then the party begins."

A few minutes later, two Asian women entered the room. All three removed their watches, coats, and rolled up their sleeves, surrounding Arham.

Arham said, "I came here to talk, not to fight."

One of them replied, "We don't care what you want. We have orders."

Arham retorted, "Ah, orders from the mother?"

Mentioning the mother caught them off guard, and they attacked. One kicked the back of his legs, another pushed him to the ground, and the third pulled out a dagger made of the same white, shiny material the queen had shown him, aiming for his heart.

Arham fought back, pushing the dagger-wielding woman into the other and grabbing the third by the neck. He stood up, still holding her, and warned, "Attack again, and I'll fight you like men."

They regrouped and attacked again. This time, Arham was ready. He threw punches and kicks, sending them crashing into furniture and walls. Though they were trained fighters, they were no match for Arham's boxing and Muay Thai skills.

When they realized they were overpowered, they grabbed broken pieces of furniture and used the metal parts as weapons. One struck Arham in the stomach, another pushed him toward a glass window, and the third rammed into him, sending him crashing through the glass.

Arham fell three floors down into the entrance lobby, landing next to the woman who had pushed him. Dazed, he noticed the dagger on the floor. He grabbed it and held it to her neck as the other women descended the stairs.

Arham stood up, using the woman as a hostage, and warned the others to stay back or he'd kill her. He dragged her away outside the building away from other sisters, then pushed her aside and said, "I want to meet your mother and make peace with her. I'm not your enemy. I mean no harm."

He slowly handed her the dagger, signalling his intent not to harm her. She took it and said, "I'll pass on the message, but it won't matter. Your fate is decided by the Sisters' Council, not the mother alone."

Arham asked, "Where can I find the council?"

She replied, "The council is a secret group. They don't even know each other personally. Their meetings are discreet, and once a decision is made, it can't be undone. Your decision has already been made. I'm sorry, but dying is your only option—if not today, then tomorrow."

She walked away, and Arham headed to the rendezvous point. A car arrived shortly after and took him away.

When Arham met Hamid, he asked about the Sisters' Council, but Hamid claimed to know nothing about it, suggesting the daughter had lied to escape. Unsatisfied, Arham demanded to see the queen, but Hamid refused, stating their task was incomplete. They had started tracking the daughters and needed to be ready to confront the mother, Leena.

Frustrated, Arham said, “Fine. I’ll ask the mother about the Sisters’ Council myself.”

Hamid ignored him, and they continued tracking the daughters.

---

* * *

Chapter 8: Mother of Monsters

The next day, the three daughters travelled to Lisbon, Portugal, via different routes. That night, they were tracked to a six-story building in the middle of the city. Arham was informed that the daughters were on the top floor, likely accompanied by the mother. He was given a communication device and a pair of shoes with a hidden compartment in the sole containing a white dagger.

Arham took the elevator to the top floor. Upon arriving, he carefully exited and approached the entrance of a brightly lit lounge. Security personnel frisked him, removing his communication device. Inside, men and women sat on couches, drinking and chatting, while loud music played and some danced.

One of the security guards escorted Arham to a private sitting area. It became clear they had been expecting him. Arham followed and was led to a corner where an elderly woman in a white robe sat. He greeted her and sat across from her, unsure how to start the conversation. The old lady sipped her drink, her eyes fixed on the dance floor.

After a few minutes of silence, Arham spoke. “Let me start by apologizing for hurting your daughters. It wasn’t my intention. I warned them they’d get hurt if they attacked me, and I repeatedly asked them to stop. I just wanted to talk, but they didn’t listen.”

The old lady finally responded, her voice calm but sharp. “I know. Now, answer one question, and I’ll tell you whatever the hell you want to know.”

Arham leaned back, surprised by her directness.

She asked, "How did you find our office in Málaga, and how did you track us here? Who's helping you?"

Arham lied, "I followed the Indian woman from Thailand."

The old lady shook her head. "Not possible. She left Thailand before you.. Don't lie. The truth will keep you alive. Your next lie could be your last words."

Arham, visibly uneasy, replied, "I came here with good intentions to make peace, and you're threatening me with hell and last words. Listen carefully, lady—this could be the last words *you* hear. If you don't make a truce with me, I'll rip the heads off you, your daughters, your sons, and everyone else in this room."

The old lady placed a hand on her ear, speaking into a hidden earpiece. "Are you sure you want me to send him in?" After a pause, she said, "Okay."

She stood and addressed Arham. "Today's your lucky day. You get to meet our mother."

Arham was shocked. "I thought *you* were the mother."

She smirked. "I'm the oldest daughter, not the mother."

She announced to the room that they were closing for the day and instructed everyone to leave immediately. She then led Arham through a series of doors into another lounge. This room had a dark interior, with soft music playing. About 40 women—all either white or Indian—sat there, including the three he had fought in Málaga.

As Arham entered, the music stopped, and the room fell silent. The women stood, staring at him, ready to fight. At the far end of the lounge, two figures sat in the shadows.

A young woman's voice called out, "Hello, boy. How are you doing?"

Arham replied, "Hello. I was doing fine until I met this old, evil lady," pointing at the oldest daughter.

The young woman laughed. "You're a funny guy, aren't you?"

Arham joked, "I guess you must be the youngest daughter. Where's your mother? Inform her of my arrival."

The room erupted in chuckles. The young woman stepped out of the shadows and said, "Young, I am. The mother, too, I am."

Arham was stunned. The woman before him appeared to be in her late twenties, beautiful and youthful. He recalled the queen's warning about the mother using her daughters for her youth but remained sceptical.

To test her, he asked, "If you're the mother, who's the other woman in the shadows?"

She replied, "I am Leena, the mother and ruler of the Indian subcontinent. The woman sitting in the shadows is Mother Grace, ruler of Europe. She doesn't trust you enough to show herself."

Arham quipped, "So, you're both part of the Sisters' Council that decided to kill me?"

Leena nodded. "Me, her, and the four other mother rulers of Africa, the Americas, the Middle East, and Russia have decided your fate."

Arham smirked. "Wow, I didn't know I was that famous. Well, here I am, and my proposal is simple: live and let live."

Leena burst into laughter, repeating, "Live and let live? Live and let live? Sorry, boy, that won't work. The decision is made, and once the council passes it, it cannot be reconsidered. But before I kill you, you must tell me who helped you find us in Spain. I need to fill the grave next to yours with that traitor."

Arham replied sarcastically, "Well, old lady, your negotiation skills are terrible."

Leena's expression darkened. "Old? Do I look old to you?"

Arham realized his mistake. By calling her old, he had revealed he knew her secret. He quickly tried to cover it up. "Stop calling me 'boy,' and I'll stop calling you 'old.'"

Leena's rage flared. She stepped back and delivered a powerful kick to Arham's abdomen. The force sent him flying across the room, crashing through a window. He fell six floors down, landing on a parked car below.

---

* * *

Chapter 9: Truce of Blades

Arham lay on the roof of the car, surprised by Leena's strength but also excited at the prospect of finally having a worthy opponent. He got up, unharmed by the fall but feeling a slight pain in his ribs from the kick. It wasn't much, but it was rare for him to feel any pain at all—the last time had been when the Vietnamese gang blew up the clinic in Thailand.

He looked up and saw Leena staring down from the broken window. She turned and shouted to her daughters, "Get me his head!"

Arham walked back to the building's entrance and waited for the elevator. When it arrived, it was filled with daughters. He stepped inside, surrounded by tense, hostile faces, and said, "Let's take the fight upstairs."

They reached the top floor, where more daughters were waiting in the lounge. Arham, though slightly nervous, was eager for the challenge. He slowly removed his shoes, revealing the hidden daggers in the soles. With a smirk, he said, "Surprise."

The daughters attacked en masse, but Arham defended himself skilfully, stabbing their limbs whenever they kicked or punched. Though cornered, he used the narrow space to his advantage, forcing them to attack from the front. One by one, the daughters retreated, bleeding and injured, while Arham remained largely untouched.

The fight turned into a bloodbath. All forty daughters were wounded, and the lounge was a mess. Just as Arham began to feel confident, Mother Grace entered the elevator carrying a golden box. She opened it, revealing a dozen white-bladed daggers. She handed them to the daughters, who regrouped, now armed with the deadly weapons.

Realizing he was outmatched, Arham quietly slipped into the elevator. "I'll be back in five minutes," he said, closing the doors.

He hurried down to the alley where a car was parked. Opening the trunk, he retrieved the white-bladed sword and replaced the daggers with it. Hiding the sword behind his back, he returned to the lounge.

The daughters were bandaging their wounds when Arham reappeared. A group stood up, holding the white daggers, ready to fight. Arham revealed the sword and said, "Ladies, I have another surprise."

The daughters froze, their confidence shattered. They looked to the mothers for guidance. Leena and Grace exchanged glances, clearly surprised.

Leena stepped forward. "You can have your truce. Let's sit and discuss the terms."

Arham followed them to the dark lounge, where the three sat alone. Mother Grace spoke first. "It's clear you're being helped by one of the mothers. Otherwise, you wouldn't have the dagger or the sword. You know more about us than you're letting on. Deny it all you want, but to enforce this truce, tell us: Why were you given these weapons and sent to us?"

Arham replied, "I was asked to kill Mother Leena. I was told it was the only way to stop the daughters from hunting me.

But I refused. I said I'd talk my way to peace instead. They didn't believe me and thought I'd have to kill or be killed, so they gave me the weapons as a last resort. And for the record, I don't even know if the one who sent me is a mother. Maybe she's just a kind person trying to help me."

Leena smirked. "Ah, it's a 'she.' Definitely a mother. A human woman wouldn't have the knowledge, and a daughter wouldn't have the courage."

Grace added, "Fine. You have your truce. We'll let you live and won't attack you anymore."

Arham raised an eyebrow. "What about the Sisters' Council's orders?"

Grace replied, "The council will see our efforts to kill you and be satisfied. The real question is which sister planned to kill Leena and went against the council's orders. She's broken the Sisters' Code and will have to answer for it."

Arham asked, "So, do I have to fight you now?"

Leena shook her head. "Rejoice, boy. You're free to go. Walk out of here and lie to the traitor mother. Tell her you've killed me. Once she knows, she'll try to finish you to erase all witnesses and protect herself from being exposed as a traitor. She used you because when one of us dies, her daughters are distributed among the others. She's probably out of daughters, and without them, she'll die."

Arham's eyes widened. "So the blood transfusion and organ donor thing is true? I thought she made it up. And you're really four hundred years old?"

Leena nodded. "Yes. And she's probably visibly older, isn't she?"

Arham said, "Very old. You must have guessed who she is by now, out of the other four mothers."

Leena shrugged. "No. I haven't met them in over three hundred years. Our council meetings are held with faces concealed. I only recognize them by their voices, and even those are altered with technology now."

Arham asked, "How are you and Grace together?"

Leena explained, "Grace came to me six decades ago, asking for access to my daughters' blood in exchange for free access to her territory in Europe. According to the Sisters' Code, we can't travel to each other's lands, so it was a good deal. Since then, I've helped her find daughters from my territories."

Arham nodded. "Okay, it's a good deal for me, but I won't help you track her. If what you say is true, I'll deal with her my way."

Leena smiled. "I haven't asked you to track her. Just go."

Arham left, knowing they'd likely follow him through surveillance to uncover the traitor's identity. He drove to the address written on a note left in the car, a house outside the city. Another note inside instructed him to wait until they came for him.

A week later, while Arham was sleeping, he heard a faint noise and woke to find Hamid standing in the dark, holding a white dagger.

Arham sat up quickly. "What are you doing here with that dagger?"

Hamid replied nervously, "I've come to take you to our queen. Let's go—we might be hunted by the daughters."

They left in another car, heading to an airbase where a private jet with covered windows waited. After hours of travel, they arrived at the same beach mansion in the desert.

---

* * *

Chapter 10: Traitor Exposed

The next morning, Hamid instructed Arham to meet the queen in the same room where they had last spoken. She was seated in the corner, gazing at the ocean, just as before. For Arham, it felt like déjà vu, but this time, he knew far more than he had during their previous meeting.

Before Arham could sit, the queen stood and congratulated him. "You've done the impossible, my son. Tell me, how did you end the evil that was Leena?"

Arham realized Leena had faked her own death and decided to play along. "It happened quickly, and it was brutal. Frankly, I don't want to talk about it. I took a life, and I'm not proud of it."

The queen smiled. "You took one life but saved millions, including your own. You should be proud. You can return to India or Thailand without worry. Hamid will arrange your travel in a few days."

Arham thanked her and left the room, his mind racing. He now understood that the queen was part of the Sisters' Council, which was how she knew of Leena's supposed death.

That night, Leena's warning kept Arham awake. She had told him he would be killed to erase all witnesses. He slept with the lights on, but suddenly, the room went dark. He heard his door creak open and saw a figure approaching slowly.

The figure lunged at him, wielding a white-bladed sword. Arham rolled away just in time, and the sword pierced the mattress. He pushed the attacker toward the window, and in the moonlight, he recognized the queen.

Arham said, "Leena told me you'd try to kill me."

The queen hissed, "What else did she tell you?"

"She said you must be out of daughters' blood to extend your life."

The queen sneered. "Well done. You've solved the mystery. Now, let me put you to sleep forever."

Arham was shocked by her agility and the absence of her Middle Eastern accent. She attacked again, and Arham, unsure how to fight back against an old woman with a sword, ran out of the house. She leaped from the mansion's balcony to the ground, landing gracefully with the sword in hand. He ended up on the dark beach, the queen chasing him with terrifying speed.

Arham ran along the beach, hoping to exhaust her. After a few miles, he stopped, breathless, and turned to see her still pursuing him, though visibly tired.

Arham panted, "You're a crazy old lady."

She replied in her Middle Eastern accent, "Help me, my son. I'm tired."

Arham shook his head. "I'm not falling for your act again."

She closed the distance between them and said, "I've slain many men of our kind and will continue until none of you remain. You'll never rule us again. Come to me and fulfil your destiny, my son."

Suddenly, headlights appeared on the beach. A car stopped beside Arham, and Leena stepped out. The queen glared at her and said, “I knew the boy didn’t have the courage to take a life.”

Leena replied coldly, “I’ll make sure you’re expelled from the Sisters’ Council for plotting to kill me. And you, Arham, will be my witness.”

The queen screamed, “No!” and hurled the sword at Arham. It struck his chest, penetrating only a few millimetres before hitting bone and falling to the ground. Arham, seeing his own blood for the first time, picked up the sword and threw it into the ocean.

The queen dove into the water to retrieve it, while Leena urged Arham into the car. As they drove away, Arham asked, “Why is the white-bladed sword so rare?”

Leena explained, “It’s made from the bones of our dead. That’s what makes it so powerful.”

Arham frowned. “Which Middle Eastern country are we in?”

Leena chuckled. “Who said we’re in the Middle East? We’re in Chile, South America. That crazy old woman was the ruler of the Americas. Her name is Seraphina. She made you think she was Middle Eastern so that, if you were captured, you’d mislead us.”

Arham leaned back, exhausted. “Now what?”

Leena replied, “Rest. We have a long journey back to Portugal, and I need to figure out how to defend you in the Sisters’ Council.”

Meanwhile, the queen Seraphina sat in the plush cabin of a private jet, her frail hands clutching a glass of drink. The plane descended toward a remote island; its lush greenery visible even in the moonlight. As the jet touched down, she was greeted by a towering, well-built man with an air of quiet authority. Around him, hundreds of women and children moved about, their lives revolving around him.

The man, one of the last surviving warriors of "the other kind," had lived in secrecy for centuries, sustaining his life through the blood of his offspring.

The queen approached him, her voice steady but laced with urgency. "You are not the alpha anymore. There is another—stronger than you. And he is coming."

The man's eyes narrowed, a flicker of fear passing through them. The queen smiled faintly. "But don't worry. I've kept your secret safe. For now."

The queen sat silently beside the last warrior, their eyes fixed on the horizon where the sun bled into the sea—two relics of a forgotten war, watching as the first shadows of the next began to rise.

---

* * *

Chapter 11: Echoes of the Two Kings

While Leena and Arham were traveling back to Portugal, Arham grew anxious and asked her to know more about the other Mothers.

Leena said, "I was part of the beginning of an era for our kind. It has lasted until now for over four centuries, but now, after meeting you, I think this era will come to an end."

Arham asked, "Why?"

Leena replied, "The rules of the Sisters' Code have been shattered. First, Queen Seraphina tried to kill me, and later I entered her territory without her permission and knowledge to save you. This has never happened in our history."

Arham laughed. "I didn't need saving. You were there for your own benefit. You wanted to know who had planned to kill you. Also, I think I am with you right now because you want me to be your witness, as you said earlier."

Leena replied, "Don't get ahead of yourself. Don't try to act smart—you don't know what you are talking about."

Arham quipped, "Then please explain."

Leena said, "Do you think Seraphina will admit that she had planned to kill me and accept her punishment, which is death according to the Sisters' Code? She will fight back, and I don't think the other Mothers will take my side. I am sure Grace will, but others will probably think politically and try to punish me too, as everyone will see their benefits—that is, the inheritance of my and Seraphina's daughters. And then there is you, who is alive and breathing. As far as I know, you, my friend, should be long dead according to the Sisters' Council decision."

Arham closed his eyes, pulled his tongue out, and jokingly said, "Here I am dead. Take a photo and send it to your Sisters' Mothers Council… whatever."

Leena said, "I call you 'boy'—I was wrong. I should refer to you as an infant because you act like one."

Arham retorted, "Look who is talking—a 400-year-old mummy who steals blood from kids she kidnaps from their parents and forces them to call you 'Mother.' Like, seriously, you are not even related!"

Leena replied, "I don't know what Seraphina has told you. I don't kidnap them—I adopt them. I pay the parents handsomely for it. What would you have done if you were in my place? You would have done the same. Extending life is something invaluable. I do it, Grace does it, and your friend Seraphina does it too. Probably the other three Mothers also do it. Extending life by buying blood is not a sin or a crime anywhere."

Arham said, "Okay, you put it like that—now it sounds reasonable. How come you know the other Mothers do take blood or not?"

Leena replied, "Well, during the initial years of our Sisters' Council meets, I advised the other Mothers to do meets in shadows or veils so we don't get the urge to meet and greet or be friendly to each other. Too much power concentrated in one place is a disaster; we had to avoid it. They accepted, but the real reason was that I had stopped aging after I discovered the blood transfusion, and they were questioning my youth every time we met. I kept it to myself as a secret for years. The other Mothers too discovered it some time later, or they would not have lived until now."

Arham asked, "What about organs? Do you steal them too?"

Leena quipped, "Rubbish! I don't need to—the blood transfusion is enough."

Arham replied, "I will be honest: you are way more convincing than Seraphina. I believe you."

Leena replied, "What else do you think I am—a witch?"

Arham said, "Oh no, I was going to say vampire."

Both laughed together.

Arham asked, "How do you convince your daughters to give blood? Why don't they share it within themselves and increase their age?"

Leena replied, "Okay, you are asking questions way out of your league, boy. I am starting to rethink my decision of saving you."

Arham said, "I am curious. Tell me—if you think you're not doing anything wrong, prove me wrong."

Leena replied, "My answer will be the same: too much concentration of power in one place will be a disaster. Two Mothers cannot rule together; it will always end in war, like it did for the Two Kings."

Arham quickly said, "That was not the answer I had wished for. By the way, what two kings are you referring to?"

Leena replied, "Buckle up and listen to history, boy. The two worst kings from among hundreds of kings in the past ended up being born in the same decade, which led to the end of an era for our kind. They brought upon a decades-long war on our kind, the likes of which were never known in our world. Kaelom—King of the East—and Xalvador—King of the West. Kaelom wanted more territory and control of Africa for slaves, and Xalvador wanted parts of Europe and beyond in the New World. Soraya, the Middle Eastern Mother, and I were warriors under Kaelom. Grace was one of the many queens of Kaelom. Seraphina was one of the queens of Xalvador, and Zalika, the African Mother, and Vasilisa, the Russian Mother, were warriors in his army.

"Both kings decided to go to war against each other, despite refusal from their councils and warriors. They openly advocated to their people that this war would be the first and last of its kind, and the victor would become the supreme leader of the world. Their egos decimated our lives and brought our kind to the brink of extinction. Seeing our brethren die, we warriors decided to broker a peace treaty mid-battle without our kings' approval. Hearing this, both kings joined and led the battle themselves.

"After a few days, both kings, along with their queens, decided to fight directly against each other's armies to end the war that same day. By nightfall, both kings were dead, along with thousands of others. Only a few hundred of our kind remained.

"Seraphina seized this opportunity and killed Xalvador's other queens to claim full power over the West. She, Zalika, and Vasilisa decided to end the tyranny they'd endured and slaughtered all loyalists. In her rage, Seraphina then killed every adult man of the opposing faction.

"News of Seraphina's murderous rage spread to the East. Kaelom's male warriors, fearing their own queens might retaliate, began killing all queens. But Grace—a fierce woman—gathered the female warriors, promising fair treatment and an end to male rule. We fought hard against the remaining men and won. By day's end, Soraya and I had earned Queen Grace's respect and, most importantly, her allegiance. That day, the Sisterhood was born.

"Grace and Seraphina later met and forged a peace treaty called the Sisters' Code. They disbanded the armies and told warriors they were free to live wherever they chose. Grace asked Soraya and me to return to our families and, for our bravery, granted us rule over our native lands. Hearing this, Zalika and Vasilisa demanded the same from Seraphina. Though reluctant, she agreed. Thus, the rule of six nations was born: two queens and four warriors, forming the Six Sisters' Council. We four warriors rejected the title of 'queen'—'Mother' fit perfectly. Doesn't it?"

Arham said, "FYI, I am not Kaelom or Xalvador."

Leena replied, "I know you're a selfless person and don't seek a fight. I like that about you… and your good sense of humor."

Arham said, "Ah, I'm flattered."

Leena's daughter announced from the cockpit, "The flight will begin its descent."

Leena got up and headed to the cockpit.

Arham asked, "Where are you going?"

Leena replied, "Well, I'm learning to fly the plane and need landing practice. Sit tight—it'll be rough."

Meanwhile, back at the tropical island…
The last warrior, Oseye—Xalvador's former army general—remained. Seraphina spent the day analyzing Oseye's offspring to find any trace of their kind.

---

* * *

Chapter: 12: The Traitor Among Us

After arriving in Portugal, Leena received a phone call from Mother Grace.

Grace asked, "Was the traitor Seraphina?"

Leena replied, "Yes. I want to meet you in person."

Grace instructed her, "Come to my castle."

Leena and Arham took a flight to Scotland, where Grace resided.

Upon their arrival at Grace's castle, Grace saw Arham and, surprised and angry, exclaimed, "What is Seraphina's warrior doing here? How dare you bring him into my home?"

Leena explained, "He is not her warrior. When I arrived in Chile, Seraphina was about to kill him. I saved him."

Grace said, "That still doesn't answer my second question—why is he in my house?"

Leena replied, "He works for me now."

Sensing the situation, Arham nodded and said, "Yes, I do."

Grace snapped, "Are you out of your mind? He is a man of our kind, and the only one I know who has lived to be a grown adult. He has to die—or the other Mothers will kill both him and us."

Leena said, "Stop overreacting, Grace. I will fake his death. They will never know."

Grace replied, "Oh, I see. Then you either kill him where he stands, or I will." She shouted to call her daughter. "Bring me the sword that hangs on the wall!"

Her daughter asked, "Which one?"

Grace responded, "The one that says *Slayer of Kings*."

Leena turned to Arham and said, "Let's go. We fly back."

Grace ordered, "Leave my territory of Europa immediately, along with your daughters."

Leena replied, "I will leave your house now, but I will not leave Spain and Portugal. I have invested a lot of time and money there."

Grace warned, "Your investments are no good if you're dead."

Leena said, "Stand by your word, Grace. I can access Europa in exchange for helping you find daughters for yourself."

Grace responded, "Fine. Limited access to Spain and Portugal, and not a step beyond. If the other Mothers find out, I'll say you trespassed into Europa without my knowledge. If necessary, I will hunt you down along with them."

Leena agreed and left with Arham, heading back to Málaga, Spain.

The next day, Leena called for a Mothers' meeting.

All six Mothers joined via an online meeting, with video turned off—only their voices audible.

Leena began the meeting, greeting them all and stating the reason:
"All Mothers, I would like to inform you, with a heavy heart, that the Sister's Code has been broken—by one among us. According to our last meeting, we decided to send one daughter from each of the six regions to inspect Arham. Upon inspection, our daughters concluded he is one of ours and must be dealt with immediately. But Seraphina acted against us all. She first attacked Arham with local gangs and made it look like my daughters had planned a hit. I would never use humans to attack one of our own—that too would violate our Sister's Code. Later, she rescued Arham, took him to South America, told him it was the Middle East, armed him, and sent him to kill me. I had to fake my own death to convince Arham of Seraphina's evil intentions. She has violated multiple codes and must be punished severely."

Seraphina responded to the accusation:
"I have never met Arham before, nor have I planned any attack on anyone. All Leena says is baseless. It is *Leena* who protected Arham and sent him to kill *me*. If anyone deserves punishment, it's her."

Leena replied, "What would I gain by killing you? Nothing."

Seraphina snapped, "Then where is the killer you claim I sent to kill you?"

Leena answered, "He's sitting beside me—and he will be my witness."

Seraphina scoffed, "There is no witness that can go against a Sister's word. You are weak, Leena. You've always failed to do what was ordained. During the terrible war, you refused to kill Oseye and let him go free. He was a traitor. He ran from *my* territory and sought refuge with you. You let him live, despite him being our common enemy."

Leena defended, "Oseye was not a traitor. He was crucial in brokering the peace treaty we made on the battlefield. He defied his king, Xalvador. He left his territory and refused to fight alongside the other generals against you, Seraphina. When he reached my territory, he chose the right side and protected us—women—from the King's loyalists. Yet, after all he did for us, you chased him out of my lands. You all know this, but I must remind you."

Zalika intervened, "Leena, it doesn't matter whether Oseye was a traitor or not. You failed your duty as a Sister by letting a man live—then and now. You're repeating history with Arham. If you had killed Oseye when you had the chance, he wouldn't have escaped and hidden from us."

Seraphina pressed, "Why are we wasting time while the man sits beside one of us? End it now before it's too late. I vote to send my army to finish the job—end both unworthy lives. Sisters, vote now, or it will be a repeat of endless wars. We'll all suffer, like before. End it now before he gathers an army to kill and enslave women of our kind."

Soraya, the Middle Eastern Mother, intervened, "Such an important decision—the ending of a Sister's life—cannot be taken in haste."

Seraphina shouted, "Weak! Weak! Grace—both your warriors are too weak! One harbors our enemy, the other doesn't even realize the danger we're in. You, Grace, are the wise one. Say what you're thinking!"

Grace declared, "Leena, you have 24 hours to kill Arham. If you fail, we will punish you with death."

Seraphina protested, "What? 24 hours? Why not now? So Leena gets to live after that?"

Grace said calmly, "She will kill the boy. We will meet again in 24 hours to decide Leena's fate. Whoever agrees, say so."

Soraya, Zalika, Vasilisa, and Leena all agreed to Grace's decision.

Zalika added, "Leena, my sister, you'd better do what was agreed. If not, I promise I'll be the first to do what is required to protect the Sister's Code. I will show no mercy."

Seraphina laughed coldly, "Well, I suppose I have to go with the majority."

Leena responded sarcastically, "Congratulations, Sera. You're very close to getting what you wanted—end me and take my daughters. My dear sisters, I look forward to seeing you again tomorrow."

The meeting ended.

Arham turned to Leena and asked, "Well, the meeting didn't go as you'd planned."

Leena smiled and replied, "Well, that can change—if I kill you now."

Arham asked, "So… are you going to kill me?"

Leena responded, "No. I have other plans."

Arham looked confused. "I don't understand. Why aren't you attacking me after everything they said? According to them, either I die, or we both do. What are your plans? Enlighten me."

Leena said with a soft smile, “Patience, dear. By tomorrow, you’ll know.”

---

* * *

Chapter 13: The Ultimatum

That night, Grace came to meet Leena in Portugal and informed her that she needed to leave the territory before tomorrow's meeting. She warned Leena to get rid of Arham immediately or risk her own end due to stubbornness.

Leena refused and said,
"I am returning, along with my daughters, to Istanbul—*my* territory. You don't need to worry about my well-being. I'm more than capable of taking care of myself, and you know that very well."

Grace replied,
"Well, then I suggest you go back and hide with your daughters deep in your forests, away from civilization. The Mothers will not stop looking until they end you. Also, what makes you think your daughters will accept a life in hiding? They enjoy luxury and opulence. There's no way they'll give all that up just to protect you."
She pointed at Arham and said,
"End him now. Stop being stubborn and listen to me—just once."

Arham said sarcastically,
"Oh, I tried to convince her too—to kill me—but she refuses to listen. She told me she has a plan."

Grace glared at Arham and said,
"You're the last person in the world who gets to have a say in this. I regret not killing you in Lisbon."

Arham responded,
"You all tried—and failed miserably."

Leena walked toward Grace, hugged her, and whispered in her ear,
"I found Oseye."

Grace, shocked, pulled back and asked aloud,
"Did you say you found Oseye?"

Leena nodded.
"Yes. Oseye. I found him on an island in the Pacific a couple of days ago—and just this morning, I confirmed it's him."

Still stunned, Grace asked,
"How did you find him? How is he still alive and hasn't crossed paths with us in all these years? Were you hiding him?"

Leena replied,
"Wait on the questions—and no, I wasn't hiding him. As I said, I only learned about him two days ago. I had asked my daughter to track Seraphina's whereabouts after I met her in Chile. I was expecting an attack from her on my return here, so I took precautions. And to my surprise, she traveled to a remote island in the middle of nowhere in the Pacific.

My daughter informed me that Seraphina met with an African male on the island—and the place seems to be a breeding program. At first, I thought it was just Seraphina being Seraphina—desperate for donors, likely experimenting—but then I dug deeper. The island is inhabited by only *one* adult male. The rest are young women and their children. And the description of that male matched only one of our kind known to still be alive: Oseye."

Grace stood silent, too shocked to respond. After a moment, she said softly,
"We are going to war—sooner than I had thought."

Leena said with frustration,
"Seriously? That's the only thing you can think of—war?"

Grace replied,
"The rise of *two* males of our kind is what I fear the most. Leena, my dear, you haven't lived long enough to witness what I have."

Leena said,
"Well, Oseye was the one who stood against war. You know that very well. And Arham is like a baby in our world."

Arham interjected,
"Baby? Are you serious?"

Grace said,
"Yet here we are—at the brink of war. And by tomorrow, it's highly likely you'll breathe your last."

Leena stated firmly,
"There will be no war. I will inform the Mothers about Oseye—then the decision can be made justly."

Grace sighed.
"I like your optimism. I want the best for you. Without your courage—and Soraya's—I wouldn't be here today."

Leena, with respect, said,
"Sleep well, my Queen. Let *me* worry about tomorrow."

---

* * *

Chapter 14: Wreckage and Reckoning

That same night, Leena and Arham took a flight to Istanbul, Turkey. East Istanbul was under Leena's territory. They returned so that, if the upcoming meeting went south, Leena would be able to protect herself better on her own land.

They arrived in the morning and drove from the airport to one of Leena's houses. One of Leena's daughters was driving, with Arham in the passenger seat and Leena sitting in the back. Suddenly, a heavy trailer from the opposite lane swerved violently into their lane and crashed head-on into the car at high speed. Almost simultaneously, another trailer slammed into the rear of the car.

The vehicle was crushed into a mangled wreck—so destroyed that no human could have survived. The passengers were not visible in the debris. Moments later, several cars arrived and blocked the road from both ends. Around a dozen female warriors emerged from the vehicles, clad in modern armor from head to toe, carrying white-bladed daggers.

They began dismantling the wreckage piece by piece. Eventually, they dragged Leena out. She was visibly injured and disoriented. One of the warriors pushed her away from the wreckage and struck her on the head.

Realizing they meant to kill her, Leena fought back, but her injuries and the overwhelming number of attackers left her defenseless. They beat her relentlessly until she could no longer stand. Two warriors held her by her arms while others stood guard. One stepped forward with a white-bladed sword and prepared to decapitate her. She ordered the others to hold Leena still as she knelt, struggling to break free.

At that moment, the crushed car groaned and shifted. Arham, forcing his way out of the wreckage, shouted in a thunderous, furious tone,
"Get away from her!"

He emerged, lifted the car engine over his head, and hurled it at the warrior poised to kill Leena. The engine struck her, sending her crashing to the ground. The other female warriors rushed at Arham. Though injured, his rage fueled him. He was struck multiple times but retaliated with even greater force.

One of the warriors lunged at him from the air, attempting to stab him with a dagger. Arham caught the blade with his palm—letting it pierce through—then punched the attacker, yanked the dagger from his own hand, and fought back with it.

Inspired by Arham's resistance, Leena fought off the two warriors holding her. Arham showed no restraint, grabbing warriors, tearing off their helmets, and slitting their throats in a blood-fueled frenzy. He killed four. Leena managed to seize the sword and killed one more.

Just then, one of the attackers shouted that Leena's daughters were on their way. The remaining warriors retreated, rushing back to their vehicles and speeding away.

Breathing heavily, Arham—wounded and exhausted—stumbled over to Leena and sat beside her on the pavement.
"Are you okay?" he asked.

Leena, still catching her breath, instructed,
"Check on the daughter who was driving."

Arham walked to the wreckage, pulled out the mangled body, checked for a pulse, and turned to Leena.
"Sorry. She's gone."

Leena, furious, screamed,
"Seraphina! I will have your head for this!"

Leena's daughters arrived at the crash site. Seeing their mother bloodied, they demanded to know what happened. Leena explained and ordered them to find and eliminate the female warriors who had attacked before they left the territory.

A group of daughters immediately left to fulfill the order.

Arham then asked,
"Why did she attack before the 24-hour deadline? Why didn't she wait until after the meeting?"

Leena rose to her feet and said,
"Let's go to the meeting and find out."

Struggling, she refused her daughters' help. She stood—then collapsed again. Her daughters rushed to support her, but she pushed them away.

Arham, watching silently, stood and approached.
"You're hurt badly. There's no shame in it."
He gently picked her up and carried her to the car, placing her in the seat.

Leena's daughters were stunned. One of them demanded,
"How dare you touch our mother without her permission?"

Arham ignored the question.
"Go get those bodies off the road before the authorities arrive."

The daughter narrowed her eyes at him, then turned and obeyed.

They returned to one of their houses in the suburbs. There, a medical team attended to Leena and Arham—cleaning their wounds and checking for concussions.

Later, they entered a room where the Sisters' meeting had already started online. One of Leena's daughters had informed the council of the attack and asked the Mothers to wait. Leena joined, beginning with an apology for her tardiness. She told them she was fine, but that Seraphina's daughters had attacked her and tried to kill her.

Seraphina responded,
"I sent my daughters to kill Arham and save you. I knew you were too weak to take a man's life. So I took matters into my own hands—ended the man's life before the meeting, and saved you in the process. Yet you remain ungrateful and blind to that."

Leena countered,
"Well, your daughters didn't even *look* for Arham. They attacked *me*, and tried to kill me with a white-bladed sword. You, Sera, have broken every Sisters' Code—and you will pay for it."

Zalika interrupted,
"Look who's talking. The one who harbors a man of our kind wants to talk about broken codes. Your time is up, Leena. Now you will face the consequences."

Leena replied sarcastically,
"Ah, that slipped my mind—Oseye. Yes, him. Sera, please enlighten everyone—*where* is he?"

Silence.

Leena repeated,
"Seraphina, where is Oseye? Are you there?"

Seraphina answered coldly,
"Say my name with respect. I am Seraphina, ruler of the Americas—not one of your daughters."

Leena smirked.
"Fine. *Queen Seraphina of the Americas*, would you care to tell us when you were planning to inform the council that Oseye has been living in your territory for the past six decades?"

Seraphina snapped,
"I will not respond to this absurdity."

Leena lied convincingly,
"Be careful, Queen. My daughters have videos of you sitting with him—chatting for hours."

Cornered, Seraphina admitted,
"He was harbored by one of *you* since the war. One of you gave him immortality. When donors became scarce in *that* Mother's territory, he left and came to me—in the 1960s. He offered to be my breeder in exchange for a peaceful life without extending his own.

But he lied. He used the donor blood of his offspring to extend his life. I wanted to inform you, my sisters, but I needed donors too. Killing him would've meant losing my only breeder. I planned to reveal his betrayal once I found another, but I never did. In desperation, I kept the secret. Please… forgive me."

Leena snapped,
"Lies. How many more, Sera? How did you survive over three centuries without a breeder?"

Seraphina hissed,
"I had many—they all died. If keeping a breeder is a code violation, then we're *all* guilty."

Leena turned to Zalika.
"Zalika, what was it you said yesterday? 'No mercy.' What happened? Cat got your tongue?"

Grace interrupted,
"This is too much. Seraphina, you were ready to kill Leena for harboring a man for a few days—yet you hid one for *sixty years*. You *both* broke the Sisters' Code.

I hereby pass a motion to vote: Leena and Seraphina will be stripped of their council seats, their territories and daughters redistributed. Both men of our kind will be executed—*together*, by us. Leena and Seraphina will live as my daughters, under my watch. They will be forbidden from extending their lives from this day forward."

Seraphina protested,
"This is unfair. Without donors, I'll barely survive a few months. And we must find the Mother who originally harbored Oseye. He never told me who it was—but we must uncover the truth."

Grace ignored the comment and called for a vote.

Zalika said,
"My Queen, I vouched for you. Now I feel betrayed. I vote *with* Grace."

Vasilisa also accepted the motion.
Seraphina and Leena rejected it.

Soraya voted no, saying,
"I want my sisters to live and rule with me—for eternity."

Grace frowned.
"That makes it 3–3. A deadlock. We must resolve this, or we risk shattering the Sisters' Code."

Seraphina offered,
"I propose we preserve the Code. I'll ensure Oseye lives out his days as a breeder, without extending his life."

Leena added,
"I will do the same with Arham."

Grace scoffed,
"So now you propose to *keep* adult males of our kind as breeders? That itself violates the Code."

Leena replied,
"Yes. That's *my* motion."

Vasilisa switched her vote in favor of the new motion.

Now 4–2.

Zalika, furious, exploded,
"So now we let them live? This is madness. I refuse to be part of this!"

Grace calmed her.
"Zalika, enough. We were at a stalemate. A new motion was proposed—and now passed, 4–2. Remember this day, sisters. The Code has been broken—and rewritten—in mere weeks.

Leena. Seraphina. This could be the beginning of the end of our rule. Or not. That depends on *you*."

Seraphina vowed,
"I will stand by my word—even if I must die for it."

Leena sneered,
"After today, everyone knows how much your word is worth."

Grace snapped,
"Enough! I've had enough of you both. You'd better stay in line—no more broken codes. I hereby declare this meeting adjourned."

***

Chapter 15: The Island Between Us

After the meeting, Grace calls Leena on the phone and tells her never to contact her or enter her territory again, or face consequences.
Leena is sad but agrees.

Leena gets news from her daughter that Seraphina's captured daughters, after interrogation, have revealed that Leena is being constantly tracked by other daughters of Seraphina.

Leena decides to fly out of Istanbul, deep into her territory, and travel to Malaysia.
The next morning, she and Arham take a private jet to Malaysia. En route, after a few hours, their plane's wing is hit by a projectile. The pilot loses control, and within minutes the plane crashes into the Indian Ocean.

Arham wakes up and finds himself inside the broken fuselage, deep underwater. He notices Leena, who is unconscious, removes her seatbelt, and swims out into the ocean with her. He holds onto a piece of the plane wing floating from the crash for some time while Leena remains unconscious. Arham notices an island in the distance. He swims toward the island with Leena. He reaches the shore and lays Leena down on the sand. She regains consciousness and spits out seawater she had swallowed. Arham thanks God that she is okay.

Leena stands up and, in anguish, says, "This is it. I will not rest till I find and kill Seraphina with my own hands."

Arham laughs and gently pushes Leena on the shoulder. "Calm down. First, someone has to find us—then you can go kill. Look around, we're on a tiny island in the middle of nowhere."

Leena looks around and says, "How can you not be serious now? I can't believe you. Either you're completely crazy, or I am—for being with you."

Arham sits down in the sand and replies, "I know people your age have bad tempers. Be patient, assess the situation we're in, and thank God that we're alive."

Leena walks away angrily from Arham and walks across the shore of the island. After a few minutes, she shows up from the other side of the shore and says, "It *is* a freaking island—a tiny one."

Arham says, "I told you."

Leena replies, "You genius, I had to make sure. There is no sign of my daughters who were flying the plane."

Arham says, "The plane broke apart mid-air. They could be anywhere."

She sits next to Arham and asks, "Why are you smiling?"

Arham says, "I'm scared too, but panicking won't change our situation. And I don't know why, but my life always takes a drastic turn every time I'm sitting on a beach, staring at the vastness of the ocean, admiring God's creation. In exchange, the ocean pushes me further inland to meet new people and new challenges. I'm starting to think of the ocean as a space wormhole—a doorway to new adventures."

Leena says, "Ah, I'm sorry— is the sun too hot for you, or is the saltwater affecting your brain? It's transformed a funny guy into a philosopher."

They both share a laugh.

Leena says, “When Grace called me yesterday, do you know what she told me?”

Arham mockingly says, “Kill him now—it’s your very last chance, now or never?”

Leena laughs, “No, she didn’t. She said, ‘The boy and you are alike—stubborn but merciful and just, always doing what’s right, no matter the consequences.’
She also said, ‘You are the bravest person I’ve ever met and the only person I can trust blindly.’”

Arham interrupts, “Didn’t I hear her telling you not to show your face to her ever again?”

Leena says, “Let me finish, will you? She said, ‘If not for this one decision of yours—helping the males of our kind survive—I would have been with you forever, guided you like I always have.’”

Arham says, “It always comes back to me being gone.”

Leena says, “I miss her already.”

Arham replies, “You can go. Promise I won’t stop you.”

Leena sarcastically says, “I’m about to—just can’t decide the mode of transport: to walk, swim, or fly.”

Arham says, “Your army will come looking for us, right?”

Leena responds, “Of course. They’ll come as soon as they know.”

Arham says, “Well, we were halfway there, and it was an eleven-hour flight. We might be on an island in my home country. In another six hours, they'll surely know we're not coming."

Leena says, "Oh, they *surely* know. The plane is off the radar. I think a couple of hours max to find us."

Arham asks, "What if your daughters back in your territory have also been attacked?"

Leena replies, "No way. Sera will not attack my daughters in my territory. I have many warriors and she knows it. She won't take the risk—not after the Istanbul slaughter, thanks to you."

Leena stands up and says, "I'll circle the island once more and look for survivors. By that time, I want you to get that coconut I see on the tree—for your queen."

Arham stands up in a rush and says, "Queen? Where? I don't see any queen."

Leena smiles and walks away to circle the island.

Arham rushes to the bushes, shakes the tree to drop a coconut, and also collects coconut tree leaves and sticks to make a makeshift tent-like structure to impress Leena.

Leena comes back and sees Arham working to build.

Arham hears her giggling and says, "Oh my queen, you've arrived early. If you had come just a little later, your room in the palace would have been ready for you to rest."

They both sit under the shade and drink coconut water, waiting for someone to find them.

Suddenly, they hear a plane and rush out of the shade, shouting and waving for help. They wave their hands at the plane, and then they hear multiple planes around them. On the horizon, multiple rescue boats are also visible.

Leena realizes it must be her daughters—but she is skeptical because the number of boats and planes is too many. A couple of rescue boats land onshore at a distance and approach them. Arham moves in front of Leena and tells her, "Let me handle this."

Leena replies, "You don't need to."

She says, "It's my daughters from the plane—but I don't know who the other women accompanying them are."

Two daughters from the plane come and greet Leena. Another woman says,
"Welcome, Mother Leena, to the Middle East. We are the daughters of Soraya, our mother and the ruler of the Middle East. Your daughters contacted us and asked for permission to conduct a search and rescue mission. We are glad to find you. Our mother has instructed us to attend to you as we would to her. She is waiting for you on the mainland of Oman."

While walking towards the boat, Arham tells Leena, "By the way, I said earlier I think we are in my home country—well, India is my home country, not Oman."

Leena replies in Hindi, "Malum hai re." (Translated to English: "I know.")

Arham, surprised, says, "You speak Hindi?"

Leena replies, "Dear, I was Indian."

Arham, shocked, says, "Why didn't you tell me before? For so long I was wondering why a white woman has an Indian name—and why a white lady is ruling over Indian territory and daughters of Indian origin."

Leena laughs and says, "Shh! I'm excited to see my younger sister Soraya after decades. I'm literally getting goosebumps."

Arham says, "Yes, me too. I hope she has a meal cooked for us—I'm starving."

---

* * *

Chapter 16: The Palace, the Past, and the Present

They are escorted to the Mainland, where they head toward a grand palace. There, they receive a warm welcome: girls throw rose petals over them, a red carpet awaits, and many daughters have come to see Leena. Leena feels a bit embarrassed, as her clothes are still covered in sand.

They are led to a dining hall with a huge table filled with food. They are invited to sit and eat.

Soraya arrives in the room, dressed in queenly attire with a crown. Leena, overjoyed, rushes to meet her. They embrace tightly and talk while hugging. Arham, seeing their seemingly never-ending hug, sits and starts eating.

After a while, they walk over to Arham.

Soraya says, "So, you're the person responsible for all the trouble my sister is in."

Arham replies, "Oh no, I'm the reason you two have met after a lifetime. Look how happy you are! Don't thank me—I'll help thank myself with the food."

Soraya smiles. "I like you."

Arham responds, "I like you and your hospitality. Thank you for the grand welcome."

Soraya says, "I regret to inform you my hospitality is for Leena. You're standing here breathing because of her. No man—human or our kind—has ever stepped foot in this palace. You are very lucky, my friend."

Arham nods. "I'm well aware of that. Thank you again."

Leena and Soraya join Arham at the table.

Leena asks, "Any information on Seraphina's daughters who took down my plane?"

Soraya replies, "I'm sorry to inform you—it wasn't Seraphina."

Leena looks surprised. "What? Then who?"

Soraya answers, "The projectile that hit your plane was fired from a naval warship in the Indian Ocean. I had it checked. It was an Egyptian warship—belonging to none other than Zalika."

Leena sighs. "Yeah, it has to be her. She was furious after yesterday's resolution."

Soraya reassures her. "Nothing to worry about. You're safe now. Feel at home and stay as long as you wish. My home is your home."

Arham says, "You two were very close, weren't you?"

Soraya responds, "Close? We were best friends—no, more than friends. Like sisters. We trained, fought, bled, and were even tortured together."

Arham reacts, "Tortured?"

Soraya explains, "Once, we were captured in one of the battles. We were beaten and tortured by Zalika."

Arham replies, "Okay, that's news to me. Keep it coming."

Soraya continues, "They ambushed one of the villages we were guarding. Leena, I, and eight other warriors were captured. We should have been dead if not for Vasilisa."

Leena adds, "Yes, Zalika was enjoying torturing us. We wouldn't have seen the next morning if not for Vasilisa. She insisted Zalika inform King Xalvador of our capture and let him decide our fate. Zalika and Vasilisa could never see eye to eye. Luckily, because of Vasilisa's insistence, we lived through the night. The next morning, she secretly released us—just to infuriate Zalika."

Arham says, "So she did it just to infuriate her—not out of mercy?"

Soraya responds, "We'll never know. We were just grateful to be away from that monster, Zalika."

Arham reflects, "Zalika sounds evil. Vasilisa changed her vote yesterday. She seems way kinder than Zalika."

Leena nods. "Kind, yes. And a formidable opponent. If Zalika is fire, Vasilisa is an iceberg. Remember, Soraya, during battles, we used to hope we wouldn't face either of them. They were ruthless and constantly competing."

Arham asks, "So you two were no match for them?"

Leena says, "Probably not. But we had Grace—our queen. Her fighting skills were unmatched—the best, without a doubt, among all the female warriors on both sides. Zalika was fierce and strong, Vasilisa was immovable, but Grace was quick and flawless. We were the limbs of Grace. Without us, she wouldn't even enter a battle. She knew we had her back and would sacrifice ourselves without hesitation."

Arham says, "Your camaraderie is admirable. But Leena, your relationship with Grace sounds complicated. I'm starting to feel guilty for messing that up."

Leena says, "I wish I could say, 'Don't worry, it's just like old times,' but this time it's different. She was visibly upset. I don't know what to do. I'm confused."

Soraya comforts her. "Don't worry. Everything will be fine. Time heals all wounds."

Leena says, "We should leave soon—back to my place. I don't want you, Soraya, to be in trouble for the decisions I made."

Soraya replies, "Trouble? Look around, Leena. No one knows you're here, and no one would dare come this deep into my territory."

Leena says, "Well, I was attacked in my territory yesterday, and over international waters today. I'm afraid I'll be attacked again—this time in yours."

Soraya smiles. "The only one who can attack you in my territory is me. And I'll protect you with my life, my sister. I've planned a sumptuous dinner for you tomorrow evening. Afterward, we'll hit the dance floor—just like old times."

Leena hugs Soraya. "Oh, dance! I love you, my sweetheart. I'll agree—on one condition: I leave first thing the morning after tomorrow."

Soraya agrees.

After the meal, Arham and Leena are shown to their separate rooms. They are given clothes to wear during their stay.

The Next Morning:

Arham wakes up and searches for Leena in the vast mansion but can't find her. A daughter informs him that she went for a walk with Soraya to the farmlands. He eventually finds them in the fields, laughing and talking. He waves, then heads back to the mansion.

That Evening:

Arham meets Leena in the corridor.

Arham says, "Somebody's been really busy."

Leena replies, "Well, we had literally centuries of catching up to do."

Arham asks, "So, you were at the farm the whole day?"

Leena laughs, "Oh no—farm in the morning, lunch at the beach house, swimming in the lake afterward."

Arham says, "Okay, I regret leaving you with her."

Leena smiles. "It's okay. I didn't miss you at all."

Arham retorts, "Of course you didn't. Next time, tell your sister to defend you from an attack."

Leena laughs. "Okay."

Later, Arham sees the household buzzing with preparations for the dinner. Decorations are being put up, and everyone is getting ready.

He finds Soraya.

Arham asks, "That's quite the celebration. Am I invited?"

Soraya replies, "Of course. Leena's friend is my friend."

Arham says, "I might need some new threads for the occasion."

Soraya responds, "Check your room, dear. We updated your wardrobe. If you don't like it, let me know. I'll arrange a chopper to take you to the city to buy whatever you like."

Arham says, "Okay, let me check my room first. Thanks."

Back in his room, Arham is surprised to find a tailor waiting with a fresh wardrobe. He chooses one outfit but thinks it's too flashy, so he selects a simpler one and wears it.

He heads to the ballroom and chats with Leena's daughters.

Then, Leena enters with Soraya. Both are dressed in exquisite gowns adorned with diamonds and pearls. All the daughters cheer.

Arham's jaw drops—he's never seen Leena in a dress before.

He walks toward her and says, "I've never seen anything more beautiful, more elegant than you. You are flawless—a timeless beauty, beyond any man's dreams."

Leena blushes. "Well, thank you very much. I appreciate your kind words. You look clean and handsome, too."

Soraya interjects, "What about me? We're literally wearing the same dress. Nothing for the host of the party?"

Arham, unintentionally ignoring her, turns to Leena. "Can you come with me for a minute?"

Leena agrees.

He takes her to his room, asks her to wait outside, and quickly changes into the flashy attire he'd initially rejected.

He steps out and asks, "Do I look better now?"

Leena smiles. "Absolutely. We're twinning now."

Arham holds Leena's hand, and they return to the party together.

During the celebration, Arham can't stop admiring Leena.

After the party, Soraya pulls Leena aside.

Soraya asks, "What's going on with you and that boy?"

Leena asks, "What do you mean?"

Soraya says, "At first, I thought he was just doing a good job looking out for you. But the way he looks at you—and the way you smile and blush—it's disturbing. You do realize you're a mother and an immortal? He's one of our kind sentenced to death—and a mere mortal. If this is some love story, end it now before you're heartbroken. Just say the word, and he won't wake up tomorrow. I'll take care of it. You know I'd move mountains for you—he is nothing."

Leena responds calmly, "Slow down. There's no love. I like being around him. He's rare—caring, funny, and fearless. I respect him as a warrior. He saved my life twice—during the Istanbul ambush and after the plane crash. I owe him. But I'm not planning to break any rules again."

Soraya says, "As you wish. But remember, he's a breeder. One day, he'll question your immortality, and you can't spin it like we do with our daughters."

Leena answers, "He already knows about the blood transfusion from our daughters—that it stops our aging."

Soraya's eyes widen. "What? How?"

Leena shrugs. "Thanks to Seraphina."

Soraya mutters, "That wretched woman. But you say there's no love—yet he's head over heels for you. Even a blind person could see it."

Leena asks, "Are you sure?"

Soraya says, "Without a doubt. He checks on you constantly—even from a distance."

Leena responds, "He does that because he thinks we might be attacked again. You're overreacting."

Soraya shakes her head. "Either you're blind, or you've secretly fallen for him and won't admit it."

Arham looks at Leena from across the room. They make eye contact, and Leena walks toward him.

Soraya murmurs to herself, "Oh my God, they're in love."

Night ends.

Next morning: Leena and Arham leave for Malaysia in a private plane gifted to Leena by Soraya.

---

* * *

Chapter 17: More Human Than Human

After reaching Malaysia, Arham moves into the guest house beside Leena's house. A day later, he makes his feelings evident to Leena.

He tells her, "I like you, and despite our past, I would like to marry you."

Leena smiles and replies, "I knew you had a certain interest in me, but marriage is for humans — and I am not one of them."

Arham replies, "You are more human than any human I know. We are all humans, just with a tiny difference."

Leena answers, "Super strength, unpierceable skin, bullet resistance, and a lifespan that spans centuries — no human comes even close. Also, marriage is for humans as its main purpose is to procreate. And FYI, we — the women of the other kind — cannot bear children. Our bodies just do not have the organs for it."

Arham says, "So you're telling me you don't deserve to fall in love or be loved because you cannot get pregnant?"

Leena replies, "Deserve, no. We are not destined for such human deeds."

Arham insists, "I'll make it simple for you: I want to marry you and spend the rest of my life with you."

Leena responds, "For how long? I will stay young, and you will grow old and die — at most, in the next 50 years."

Arham offers, "Well, you could stop with your blood transfusion and grow old with me."

Leena says, "Grow old and die? That is so selfish."

Arham retorts, "Look who's talking about being selfish. You and your five sisters lie to all the warrior daughters about being special and immortal, while you secretly collect blood from another batch of daughters, you're breeding solely to fulfill your selfish goal of staying immortal."

Leena calmly explains, "We do not harm them. We borrow — in exchange for all the luxuries provided to them in the world. There is only a small amount of blood that can be taken and used for transfusion. It can barely support us six, given the low population of our kind. We've kept it under wraps for the good of our world — or else imagine all the daughters fighting for limited blood. Our kind would be extinct within months."

Arham replies, "Agreed on that. But what about the males of our kind? You harm them by ending their lives early."

Leena says, "Well, that decision isn't mine alone. I'm part of the council — all decisions are made by vote, as you know very well by now."

Arham asks, "So my feelings for you are one-sided?"

Leena says, "It's not that simple. It's complicated. Let some time pass, then I'll ask the council to reconsider your future. If they allow transfusion for you, then you may wife me."

Arham scoffs, "Now you want me to be part of your evil, selfish version of what you call life?"

Leena responds, "What is it that you want? I genuinely can't comprehend, seriously."

Upset, Arham says, "Just forget that I asked."

Leena nods, "Okay. But if you really love me, one day you will change your mind."

Arham asks, "Until then?"

Leena laughs and replies, "Till then, I stay young and you grow old — and one day, when you look in the mirror and realize what a mistake you made, I'll be waiting for you."

Arham frowns, "All this is funny to you, isn't it?"

Leena replies playfully, "Well, when you stop being funny — which is rare — I have to lighten the mood."

They both share a laugh.

Leena says, "To make you happy, I've opened a bank account with some funds for you, as a gift of appreciation for saving my life."

Arham says, "A thank you would have gone further than some materialistic things."

Leena replies, "Save me once more, and next time I'll thank you. For now, please manage with ten million dollars transferred into your account."

Arham gasps, "Did you say ten million dollars? Well, in that case, your thanks can wait till later."

Leena chuckles, "That's what I thought. Spend wisely, dear."

Arham grins, "Wise is my middle name."

Arham receives his bank account details from one of the daughters. He checks the funds online on his mobile. The first thing he does is buy a laptop and create a spreadsheet to plan his spending.

A few days later, Leena watches Arham driving a brand-new hatchback. She scoffs and says, "Ten million, and you buy *this*? I thought you'd get a luxury car or a sports car. Never took you for a stingy type."

Arham replies, "My dear, it's a smart investment. It's Japanese and reliable. Besides, I have your fleet of cars to use. This one is for personal use only — or during emergencies, in case you decide to throw me out of your mansion. The town is quite far for a taxi. I did, however, rent a sports car for a day to fulfill that dream."

Leena laughs. "Okay. Anything else you've bought?"

Arham opens the rear door and pulls out some new bridal clothes and jewelry.

He says, "This is from me to you, my dear."

Leena frowns playfully, "Are you gifting me things with the money *I* gave you to spend on yourself?"

Arham smiles, "No, I am gifting the most beautiful woman in the world the clothes and jewelry I'd love to see her wear. Not that it will enhance your beauty — but the clothes will look better when you wear them."

Leena blushes. "Wow. No one has ever been so nice to me. Don't tell me you spent it all on this?"

Arham reassures her, "Oh no, this is not even one percent of the money. I sent one million each to my parents in India, and to my coach Mr. Lin and his daughter Fa Ying. Another million I've planned to invest in properties in India and Thailand for leasing, which will take care of their daily expenses. I gave one million to charity back in India. The remaining five million — I plan to buy a house for *us* to live in after marriage, and later start a business."

Leena smiles and is at a loss for words. "A house after marriage is okay, but I am *never* sitting in that car of yours."

Arham jokes, "How dare you belittle my brand-new car!"

Leena smirks, "Exactly — *little* is the word I was looking for."

Arham laughs, "Now you *have* to sit in the car."

He grabs Leena's hand and gently pulls her towards the car.

Leena playfully quips, "Stop! If my daughters see this, they'll disown me. I'll be a commoner — like you!"

Arham says, "Like I care. If they see, it's for the best. Then we can get married earlier — without your daughters giving me death stares all the time."

Arham makes her sit forcibly in the car. Leena tells her daughters not to follow them.

They take a drive around the town and end up on the beach in the evening.

Sitting on the sand, watching the waves crash onto the shore, Arham asks seriously, "Are you okay? I hope you're not upset that I forced you into the car."

Leena replies softly, "I'm good. I've never been better. Thank you, dear, for coming into my life."

Arham smiles, "You're welcome." He adds jokingly, "You can thank me like before — with more money, of course. Just saying, I'm not pushing."

Leena laughs, "Money is something I have an unlimited amount of. It's been collected for over 300 years. The amount of wealth I own is unfathomable. I've literally forgotten the number of properties I own. I had to hire property managers — and now I've forgotten how many of *them* I hired across my territories.

Have you heard humans boast about generational wealth? Mine is on another level. I call it 'Ice Age money.' A few years ago, I stumbled upon an investment I had made over a century ago and completely forgotten. It's now worth *trillions.* I thought it had gone extinct — but a megacity was built around it, and I practically own the land of an entire country.

About a decade ago, I decided to survey all my investments. It took over six months, and I left it midway — it was too frustrating and pointless. I just have too much of it."

Arham sits silently, shocked, mouth open. He breathes deeply and says, "If you're a trillionaire, you must be the richest person in the world. Don't you think you should digitize your investments and give more to the needy?"

Leena replies, "What needy? All my daughters live in luxury, and other mothers are financially well-off too."

Arham clarifies, "I meant charity to *humankind* — the ones who are the majority in the world, remember?"

Leena responds, "Oh yeah, *them.* I do have multiple trusts managed by my daughters. I do enough for them — in exchange for nothing."

Arham asks, "Why do you regard them as inferior?"

Leena says, "Because they are. Send me an entire human army, and I'll crush them alone."

Arham smirks, "In that case, I defeated you and your army in Lisbon — so you must be lower than me. I'm superior, but I don't talk to you like that. You should be humble."

Leena scoffs, "Defeated me? Oh please, I had pity on you. You don't regard me as inferior, but look how you treat my daughters. You never do what they ask — always the opposite."

Arham grins, "That's a different situation. They hate me, and I enjoy watching them rage when I get more importance than them."

Leena rolls her eyes, "Oh yes, they hate you so much that they've told me multiple times: just let us know when he's no longer welcome so we can get rid of him for good."

Arham laughs, "That's interesting. What did you say?"

Leena replies coldly, "I said: Don't even dream of harming him. He's mine. And if anyone kills him, it'll be me — knife, straight to the heart."

Arham smirks, "Ah! I'm relieved now. I'm safe from them. And *you* — you can't kill me even if you try."

Leena raises an eyebrow, "Oh? And why's that?"

Arham replies, "You owe me, remember?"

Leena laughs, stands up, and starts walking towards the car. "Let's head back. I've never been off the radar this long —

my daughters are probably panicking and imagining ways to kill you."

They head back.

---

* * *

Chapter 18: Love Against the Law

A few months passed.
Arham was now well settled in Penang, Malaysia. He had bought an apartment to stay in and was managing Leena's businesses. Arham and Leena spent most of their days together, either working or enjoying leisure activities.

One day, Arham was seated at a café in one of Leena's business complexes when a huge man of African descent came and sat opposite him at the same table. The man extended his hand for a handshake and asked,
"How are you doing?"

Arham replied,
"I'm doing fine. Do I know you?"

The man responded,
"You would know me. I was mentioned in the Sisters' Council meet, which you were a part of. I've heard a lot about you. I'm Oseye—one of your kind and a friend of Leena."

Arham said,
"Last I heard, you were on an island breeding babies for that witch Seraphina. So what brings you here?"

Oseye shrugged,
"Well, I stayed on that island for far too long. I got fed up and decided to take a world tour, which was overdue. That witch was actually happy to see me go—I don't know why."

Arham smiled,
"Would you like to order something to drink or eat?"

Oseye replied,
"Sure, whatever you're having."

Meanwhile, Leena was informed by one of her daughters that Oseye had stopped being tracked after the last Sisters' Council meeting. He had suddenly shown up at the Malaysia airport a week ago and had been following Leena and Arham for a few days without trying to meet her. The daughters, having perceived him as no threat, chose not to inform Leena to avoid troubling her. But once Oseye met Arham, they notified her.

Leena, upon hearing this, scolded her daughters and rushed to the café, worried Oseye might pose a threat to Arham.

When she arrived, breathless from hurrying, she was surprised to see both men eating and sharing a laugh. She was astonished to witness them talking cheerfully about their fights with the daughters and the other mothers.

Leena slowly walked up to them, caught her breath, and said,
"Oseye, what are you doing here?"

Oseye replied,
"That is not the way to greet an old friend."

Leena sat beside them and joked,
"Did I miss the fight?"

Arham grinned,
"No, we haven't started yet. We were waiting for you, my love."

Oseye raised an eyebrow, surprised,
"What did you just call her—'my love'?"

Leena, pointing at Arham, replied,
"This guy imagines a lot."

Oseye chuckled,
"The twinkle in your eyes says a lot more than you let on, Leena."

Leena shifted the tone,
"Enough. Now you answer—why are you here, and how did you find me?"

Oseye answered calmly,
"I'm here to thank you for saving my life. And I found you with the help of our mutual friend."

Leena raised an eyebrow,
"You're four hundred years late to thank me, my friend. I hate Soraya for this—she likes to surprise me, but this one caught me off guard. I thought you two would be at each other's throats."

Arham smiled,
"We are men of our kind, not like the other ones who fight over petty issues."

Leena joked,
"How dare you say that to your queen—and talk lowly of the other mothers."

Oseye smiled in disbelief,
"I can't believe what I'm seeing—Leena, you and Soraya are happy? I've only known us all fighting and suffering through war. Now you're queens ruling vast territories by yourselves?"

Leena nodded,
"Yes, indeed. It's not like the old times anymore. The Sisters'

Council has successfully avoided wars among our kind for centuries now."

At that moment, Leena's phone rang. A message popped up: "Seraphina has called for a Council meet at 10 a.m. tomorrow."

The Next Morning – Council Meet

All mothers assembled.

Grace asked,
"Seraphina, why have you called this meeting on such short notice?"

Seraphina responded coldly,
"Leena broke the Code again and lured Oseye away from my territory. I've been wrongly accused many times, while Leena repeatedly breaks the Code and mocks the Sisters' law. This time, I won't rest until she is punished severely. And whoever votes for her will be seen as equal to her."

Leena stood up,
"I just met him yesterday. In fact, I received the meeting notification while I was with him. He traveled on his own will. As he left from Seraphina's territory, it was *her* responsibility to stop him if it was against the Code."

Seraphina lashed out,
"Lies! You had him tracked for months and then took him away. You don't want me to have a breeder. Sisters, today she plots against *me*, tomorrow it will be *you*. She now harbors two adults of our kind. We are in imminent danger. She should be dealt with immediately!"

Leena tried to reason,
"You've gone crazy, Seraphina. I have no intention of

harming anyone. According to Oseye, he was allowed to travel to my territory with the help of your own daughter."

Seraphina sneered,
"Lies, lies, and more lies! She's planning something big. Once I'm gone, she'll finish off all of you."

Zalika interjected,
"Leena, your actions speak louder than words. You, Arham, and Oseye must go. We are out of patience. You're warned in every meet, yet you break the Sisters' Code repeatedly—without consequence."

Grace added,
"I agree. Leena is no longer the warrior she used to be."

Soraya spoke up,
"Why do we always rush to conclusions without hearing both sides?"

Seraphina snapped,
"Because of your vote last time, the traitor within us survived. Not this time. Today, I, Vasilisa, Grace, and Zalika are the majority."

Soraya countered,
"Then Seraphina should also be punished for letting her breeder travel—knowingly or not. He was *her* responsibility."

Grace intervened,
"Enough of Leena and Seraphina's fights. I suggest, to avoid mass deaths and further power struggles, Leena and Seraphina fight a duel to the death and end this once and for all."

Leena nodded,
"I accept, on one condition—if I win, Arham and Oseye live."

Grace replied,
"You're not in any position to place conditions. Seraphina, do you accept?"

Seraphina said sharply,
"No, I don't. I am weak and not young anymore. If I were in my youth, I'd have finished Leena long ago."

Zalika stood up,
"I will fight on behalf of Seraphina and put an end to this."

Seraphina smiled proudly,
"My brave warrior. You are as courageous as I remember. I accept—on the condition that Zalika fights for me."

Grace declared,
"Good. If anyone objects, speak now or remain silent. We will meet next week. I will share the location for the duel."

***

Chapter 19: Love in the Shadow of Death

It's the day of the duel. Soraya and Zalika are hosting the event. All mothers—except Vasilisa—gather on a tiny island in the middle of the Indian Ocean for the fight. A small section of the island has been cleared of trees and bushes for the battleground.

Soraya welcomes everyone. As per the agreed terms, no daughters are allowed—only mothers are permitted to witness the duel, as they do not want their daughters to see them hurt or vulnerable. Arham and Oseye have also accompanied Leena to the duel. Upon seeing them, Seraphina questions co-host Soraya about their presence when even daughters are banned.

Soraya replies, "If Leena loses, we can end the whole matter here and now."

Hearing this, Seraphina laughs and phones her daughter, instructing her to prepare two more body bags.

All five mothers gather, and Zalika and Leena are prepared, dressed in traditional armor from centuries ago. Arham sees Zalika for the first time and is impressed by her tall, muscular physique. He turns to Leena and asks to fight on her behalf.

Leena shuns him and says, "A female warrior cannot be replaced by a male. That would be outrageous."

Suddenly, Grace enters the arena, also armored up. Leena walks up to her and says, "You don't need to be in armor to see me win."

Grace replies, "You are a courageous, trustworthy warrior, but no match for the brutal force of Zalika. If anyone could beat her, it would only be me."

Leena retorts, "First you put me in a duel to the death, and now you want to fight instead of me? What is wrong with you? Why are you doing this to me?"

Grace does not reply and walks past her, announcing to everyone that she will fight in Leena's place. Leena interrupts and says, "I don't need your help, nor do I allow you to do this. So stand back and witness."

Arham goes to Leena and pleads with her to let Grace fight. He reminds her that she once told him Grace was the best of the warriors and tries to convince her.

Leena refuses and says, "If she really wanted to fight for me, she would've done it before today. Not now."

Arham asks, "And what if you lose?"

Leena replies, "Don't worry. I will win."

Both warriors get ready. Zalika shouts in aggression, holding two white-blade swords. Leena holds a sword and a shield. Grace announces the rules of the duel:

"The winner will be the one left alive. Whoever wins retains her territory. The loser will forfeit her daughters, her territory, and her life. If Leena loses, Arham and Oseye will also be executed immediately."

Arham is distraught, knowing his fate will be decided while he stands idle.

He tells Leena, "I don't know how I'll control myself if I see you get hurt. The last time I saw that was in Istanbul. I lost control and killed Seraphina's daughters."

Leena replies, "Don't be naïve. If you interfere, all five mothers are bound by the Sisters' Code to hunt us down. At least now, we have a fair chance."

Arham holds Leena's hand tightly and says, "Let me fight. I'll fight instead of you. I'll take on all of them if I must. Just don't go."

Leena gently tries to pull her hand away. "Let me fight. Either I win with honor or lose with my head held high."

Arham refuses to let go. "I love you. I don't know how to let you go into this."

Leena releases her hand and says, "I love you too. If I win, I'll marry you. I promise."

Arham smiles. "Now you'll win this fight—I know it."

Leena smiles back and walks backwards toward Zalika, locking eyes with Arham.

Seraphina scoffs, "Look, sisters—you are witnessing the shortest love story ever."

Arham glares at her. "Whether Leena wins or not, I won't die without taking you down."

Seraphina snaps, "Let the fight begin! This island is getting too noisy—we need to lessen the crowd."

Leena and Zalika face each other. The air is tense; no one has seen them fight in centuries. Grace signals the start. Zalika charges forward, leaping into the air. She attacks—Leena blocks one sword with her shield, but the other blade slips past and slices her knee. First blood drawn within seconds.

Zalika laughs mockingly. "This is the blood you took before us. I'll drain every drop from you and erase you from history."

Leena advances and bashes Zalika with her shield. While Zalika defends with both forearms, Leena swings and slashes Zalika's side. Zalika screams in pain, drops both swords, and rams into Leena, kicking the shield. Leena falls, losing her sword.

Zalika grabs the shield, hurls it away, and jumps on Leena, unleashing a flurry of punches. Leena struggles to defend herself—Zalika is too strong, too heavy. Leena is nearly unconscious.

Still atop her, Zalika grabs a nearby sword and raises it to strike the final blow.

Arham rushes in and tackles Zalika off Leena. Zalika screams and attempts to attack him. She raises her sword to swing, but Arham grabs her wrist and kicks her knee. She cries out in pain and drops to her knees. He lifts her and slams her head into the ground, knocking her out cold.

Grace and Soraya are shocked. Grace radios her daughters, ordering them to come immediately. Soraya also radios in for her and Leena's daughters.

Seraphina seizes a sword and charges at the unconscious Leena, but Oseye intercepts and wrests the weapon from her. Arham, furious, charges toward Seraphina, who flees into the woods.

He pats Oseye's back and picks up Leena, carrying her toward the helicopter.

Leena opens her eyes, sees Arham carrying her, and says, "Put me down. I can walk."

Arham replies, "Rest, my dear. You're safe now."

At the helipad, they find Grace blocking the way, sword in hand.

She declares, "Many generations ago, two leaders rose among us. They crowned themselves kings and brought a lifetime of misery. When I was younger, I could have stopped them—but I showed mercy. That mistake cost us everything. Today, I won't repeat it. You two will not leave this island alive."

Oseye replies, "You're mistaken. We're not them. You were wrong then, and you're wrong now."

Grace lunges at Oseye. He dodges—he's unarmed.

Arham places Leena inside the helicopter.

Soraya arrives and says, "This is not the time. We'll act later, together."

Grace ignores her and demands, "Give them swords. Let them fight back."

Soraya hands them swords and says, "I refuse to fight. I don't want to rush into war."

Grace turns to Arham and Oseye. "Who wants to die first?"

Arham charges with the sword but is outmatched. He loses his weapon. Oseye jumps in to protect him but is soon injured and disarmed.

Leena sees them struggling and steps out of the helicopter.

"Kill me instead. Let them live," she pleads.

Grace, surprised, asks, "Why? What do you owe them?"

Leena replies, "They've done nothing wrong. Arham saved my life twice—now three times. And while Zalika tried to kill me, you stood back and watched. I owe Arham everything."

Grace growls, "My sword will not leave this island without blood."

Leena's daughters arrive, standing between Grace and their queen.

Grace shouts, "Fight me like a man, Arham!"

Arham answers, "Then drop the sword. Let's fight with hands."

Grace agrees. She throws down her sword and commands her daughters to do the same.

Then she snarls, "Daughters—attack this man. Rip him apart limb by limb."

But Arham smiles. Before they can surround him, he charges. A barrage of punches sends many of them flying. In a whirlwind, he disables over fifteen of Grace's daughters.

He stands before Grace. "I'm waiting."

Grace, unsure, watches as Arham overpowers her daughters with raw strength and speed.

She turns to Leena. "How do I end this? If you all leave alive, Seraphina and her warriors will call for war."

Arham growls, "We don't care. Let them come—we'll give them the war they want."

Seeing the tides turned, and with Leena now standing beside Arham, Grace decides to let them go.

They all return to their respective territories.

****

Chapter 20: Her Yes Echoed in War

The same night, Zalika calls for a sisters' online meeting for the next morning.

At the morning meet, Zalika starts by saying, "I have been betrayed by my sisters. I fought fair and was stabbed in the back while an outsider attacked me in the battle. You all were mere spectators while I was attacked unfairly. I hereby have decided to leave the Sisters' Council and not be a part of it anymore."

Seraphina replies, "You don't have to leave. The one leaving will be Leena. It is time we all gather and attack Leena and take over her territory, as she broke the rules of the duel."

Grace remains quiet.

Soraya says, "Let's take a vote."

Seraphina snaps, "Vote for what? She has to pay for the mistake she's done. There is no vote now."

Grace says, "If anyone needs to be out of the council, it has to be Leena. A vote is not necessary. For now, I do not want a fight anymore with anyone. If any of you want to attack her, go ahead—I won't come in the way."

Seraphina responds, "Okay then. Zalika and Vasilisa, prepare your armies. We attack her immediately."

Zalika replies, "I do not want to fight anymore, especially when I know no one has my back."

Vasilisa says, "I am also pretty occupied within my territory. I will not be able to join you in battle."

Leena says, "Looks like it's just you and me, Seraphina. When are you arriving so I can keep your grave dug up in advance?"

Seraphina growls, "That's it. From now onwards, I will also let my breeders outgrow and fight my battles."

Soraya quips, "You already did, don't you remember?"

Seraphina snaps, "Curse you, Leena, and curse you, Soraya. May your breeders kill you." She leaves the meeting.

Leena says, "I apologize to you all. I wish we could finish the meet on a high note. I hope one day we will make amends. I promise both Arham and Oseye will never harm you in the future. If they do, I will be the first to chop their heads off."

All leave without replying, except Soraya.

Leena thanks Soraya for her support and for having her back.

Soraya tells her, "I don't want thanks. I want an invitation to your territory. I welcomed you to mine—am I not welcomed to yours?"

Leena replies, "Anytime, my dear, anytime. Just fly out of yours now if you want."

Soraya says, "Okay, see you soon."

After the meeting, Arham tends to Leena's wounds from the fight. While bandaging her, he says, "Someone promised to marry me yesterday if she survived the fight."

Leena starts laughing but winces in pain from her facial wound and replies, "I said I would marry you if I won. I survived the fight but did not win."

Arham says, "In my book, surviving is winning."

Leena says, "I'm sorry. I cannot. I am a woman of my word."

Arham replies, "I beat up an army for nothing. Just tell me—what do I have to do to wife you?"

Leena smiles softly. "Nothing, my dear. I will stop blood transfusion and allow you to marry me."

Arham jumps in joy. "Did you just agree to marry me?"

Leena says, "Yes, I did."

Arham holds her hand. "I take you as my wife and vow to live with you till eternity—by blood transfusion, as you wished. I realize I was wrong. Why do you need to shorten your life because of me, my dear?"

Leena smiles and hugs Arham.

In the coming weeks, a grand wedding is planned. Soraya and Grace are invited to the wedding.

Both of them attend, and Arham and Leena are married in Penang, Malaysia.

Arham and Leena live happily for a few months—until they have an uninvited guest.

One early morning, Arham wakes up from bed as he sees a shadow behind a curtain. He moves the curtain away to find a woman standing there.

Leena, still lying on the bed, sees the woman, suddenly sits up, and says in surprise, "What is she doing here?"

Arham asks, "Who is she?"

Leena replies, "She is the Iceberg I told you about—Vasilisa."

End of Part 1: The Rise

Authors note:

Thank you for buying and reading my book. Your feedback is warmly welcomed at **theotherkind.novel@proton.me**.

I am not a writer by trade, but I've always loved good stories. Since childhood, I dreamed of writing one myself, but I never found a complete idea compelling enough to convince *me*—and I am, admittedly, my harshest critic. This book simmered in my mind for over a decade before I finally put pen to paper in February 2025 and finished it in May 2025. The entire story—characters, plot, twists—existed fully formed in my imagination, polished over years until I felt it was truly unique, with characters worth rooting for and a plot strong enough to share.

What pushed me to write? Frustration! As a lifelong fan of superhero tales and love stories, I grew tired of waiting for fresh, exciting stories. So I channelled that energy into crafting my own adventure. Writing this book has been an absolute joy, and I hope you feel that passion leap off the page.

Your feedback matters—both praise and constructive critiques are welcome (though I ask for brevity!).

A quick heads-up: On the day I published *Part 1*, *Part 2 is already half written*. If you loved *Part 1*, brace yourself—*Part 2* doubles down on surprises and breakneck action. Follow me on Instagram @theotherkind.novel for latest updates.

Once again, peace and love to my fellow humans.

Regards,
The Other Kind

9 789334 398342

Printed at Repro India Ltd.